TAKE
ME
there

TAKE ME THERE
Copyright © 2018 M.C. Decker

Cover Design:
Michele Catalano, Michele Catalano Creative
www.michelecatalanocreative.com

Cover photo:
Jean Woodfin, JW Photography and Covers
www.facebook.com/jwphotogjw

Cover Models:
Wade Hayes and Deanna Ruge

Interior Design and Formatting:
Christine Borgford, Type A Formatting
www.typeaformatting.com

TAKE ME

ME

there

M.C. DECKER

dedication

To Christina Rhoads for being my biggest cheerleader and for ultimately pressuring me into writing this book in record time—even if I may not have slept for weeks. Now, pass me the wine! Cheers! Love you, Lady!

ASHLYNN
Present Day—Three months later

*D*RESSED IN ALL black, I stood behind a large oak tree, watching as the last of the mourners retreated to their cars. The shadow of my breath danced before me in the crisp, late November air.

My parents were the last to leave, offering their condolences to Parker, my ex, and his sister, Vanessa. The two siblings were left alone in the rural cemetery to say their final goodbyes. Vanessa's sobs echoed through the barren trees as Parker kneeled on the freshly covered grave.

Just because I wouldn't allow myself to shed a tear for Kyle Flynn, it didn't mean that I didn't deeply hurt for Parker and Vanessa. They'd already buried both their parents and now they were saying goodbye to their brother. Even though Kyle was ten years older than Parker and nearly thirteen years older than Vanessa, the three got along, more than just siblings, but also as best friends. There was a time when I'd fit into their little squad.

When Parker called to tell me the news of Kyle's passing, I was more than a little shocked. Truthfully, I tried not talking about Kyle–especially not with Parker. Just his name left me feeling guilty and afraid. I wasn't quite sure how to react, but I offered my sympathy for my ex-husband's sake. When he asked if I'd make it to the service, I quickly hunted for an excuse and told him I'd be out of town for a work conference.

I hadn't lied to him. I wasn't planning on going at all, but I guess I had to see it for myself—the casket, the grave, the final resting spot of Kyle Flynn.

Biting my bottom lip, I refused to shed a single tear. You aren't going to let him take you there again, I kept repeating to myself. *Not now. Not ever.*

After several minutes, Parker and Vanessa got up and walked hand-in-hand back to the car. I waited as Parker brushed the newly fallen snow from the windshield before getting into the car and driving off.

Finally, alone in the cemetery, I walked over to the gravesite, my heels crunching in the snow. Momentarily, I regretted coming alone. My parents would've been a shoulder to cry on, but they didn't know the whole truth. I'd told them the same lie as I'd told Parker. As far as they knew, I was hundreds of miles away in south Florida.

I'd made a decision all those many years ago to keep my secret. As a teenager, I thought my parents might've blamed me even though I knew now that wouldn't have been the case. But, I couldn't tell them now. My mother would never forgive me for keeping this secret from her for so long. And then there was also Parker. If he would've ever known the side of Kyle that I'd known, it would've broken him. I never told him my version of Kyle and I never could.

I had wanted to tell Carson. I wished he was standing at my

side, but instead I ran from him. I'd come very close to telling him everything while wrapped in his arms as I desperately wanted to give him all of me. I wanted him to finally be the one to take me there, but in the end, I was too afraid–I was always too afraid.

The secrets I'd kept for all those years were now buried with Kyle Flynn and that's where they would have to remain–forever.

one

ASHLYNN
Twelve years ago

EXHALING SHARPLY, I focused on the clock tick off seconds as Parker and I waited in our new therapist's office.

"I'm not sure if this was a good idea," I said, my voice trembling. "I don't think I'm ready for this, Parker. Please just take me home."

"Ash, we agreed," he said, reaching for my sweaty palm.

"No, you agreed," I snapped, jerking my hand away. "I just don't think I'm ready to tell my darkest secrets to a stranger."

"You won't tell me, so what other option do we have? Are you just ready to give up? Throw away everything we've built? I love you, Ashlynn, but I can't keep doing this with you," he yelled, raking his fingers through his hair.

"You knew when you married me that I was far from perfect. You knew I was carrying around a truckload of baggage. I told you then that it wasn't a good idea, but you just kept on asking. You gave me no other choice but to finally give in."

Parker let out an audible sigh, telling me that my words had stung him. It was never my intention to hurt him, but he'd left me no other choice. If he'd just listened when I'd told him I couldn't marry him.

"No one is perfect, Ash, and everyone has baggage. I just wish you would let me in on your secrets because then maybe I could make it easier for you. Maybe things would get easier for us. I just want to be with you. I want to hold you. I want to protect you and I want to love you. Please, Ash, just let me love you," Parker nearly begged. "It hasn't always been like this for us. Remember when we were young? Things were so easy then. Something changed between us and you won't talk to me about it."

"We were just kids, Park. Of course, things were easy back then. Our biggest concern was what time the ice cream truck would drive through the neighborhood," I said in frustration. "There's nothing I want to talk about. Can you just let it go?"

Just as I was about to get up and leave there was a light knocking on the door. "May I come in?" a female voice requested.

"Yes," Parker responded, eyeing me suspiciously.

"Hello, I'm Dr. Joleen Reynolds. You must be Mr. and Mrs. Flynn," the woman said, walking into the office.

"It's a pleasure to meet you, Dr. Flynn. We've heard nothing but good things. Right, Ash?" Parker said, looking in my direction.

"Mmmhmm," I muttered, just hoping to get this over with as quickly and painlessly as possible. At that moment, I was almost certain that a trip to the gynecologist would be more pleasant.

"What brings you both in to see me today," she asked, flipping open our chart.

Looking back toward the clock, I listened as Parker began to rehash our story with Dr. Reynolds.

This was going to be the longest hour of my life . . . But, if I could fake so many orgasms over the years then I could certainly fake this too. I just hoped that I could fool Dr. Reynolds as easily as I'd tricked Parker for so long.

My husband definitely didn't deserve this and I didn't deserve him.

two

ASHLYNN
Present Day

"**O**H FUCK, BABY. I'm almost there. Your pussy feels so good." Jeff screamed as he pumped in and out of me. Or, was it Jarrod? Fuck, I don't even know this guy's name. What was I doing? I'd become so desperate to find the "Big O" that I'd settled for a one-night stand with a random stranger. My mother would be so proud.

"I'm coming," Jeff–yeah I'm going with that–screamed, as he thrust into me one last time. Well, good for you, buddy. At least that means that one of us got a tiny bit of enjoyment from this arrangement.

Before I had a chance to roll over and sneak off into the bathroom, Jeff turned to his side, pulling me into his chest. Fuck me–Jeff was a cuddler. When we left the bar over four hours ago, I hadn't agreed to a slumber party.

"As much as I'd love to spend more time wrapped in your arms, I have to be to work in just a few hours," I lied, hoping Mr.

One-Night-Stand would take the hint.

"I'll just stay here then," Jeff said, pulling me closer. He really was fucking clueless. It was looking like I had a stage five clinger on my hands.

"I really don't think that's a good idea. My neighbor is really a nosey old bag, and I'd hate for her to see you doing the walk of shame in the morning," I lied again. I'd have to apologize to Mrs. Sweet later. She really was as sugary as her last name suggested.

After several more minutes of Jeff trying to snuggle his way into my blackened heart, he finally wised up and saw himself out. Reaching under the bed, I pulled out my golden toy chest. Don't judge, every woman over the age of twenty-five should have a box containing all her vibrating treasures.

I needed to at least try to release the pressure building in between my thighs, even if I knew it'd be all for nothing. I was always buying the newest vibrator–each bigger and more powerful than the last. And, each claiming to give you the most intense orgasm of your life. Quite frankly, I wasn't looking for the most intense. At this stage of the game, I'd settle for just a tiny, little ripple.

With all the toys under my bed, and with more men in my bed, I looked like a sex goddess–a nympho, maybe even a slut–but as they say, looks can be deceiving. I wasn't any of those things. I was just a liar, a fake, and a fraud. The demons of my past would always haunt and torture me. My ex-husband could attest to that.

THE HOSPITAL'S SLIDING glass door creaked as it slid open. Dashing through, I glanced down at my watch hoping I still had time to grab a latte and a muffin before my first appointment arrived. No such luck. Since Jeff spent more time in my bed than I'd anticipated, I'd slept through my first alarm, leaving me no extra time to stop at the coffee shop around the corner. I wasn't the biggest fan of hospital coffee; it was sludgy and more like oil than java, but at this point, anything with caffeine would have to suffice. I'd somehow have to survive the day without my tall hazelnut mocha with an extra shot of espresso.

"Oh my god, please tell me my first appointment is running late," I asked Brad, as I scurried past the nurses' station. "I need coffee! I'll even take it black. I'm so desperate!"

"Mmmm, afraid not, Ash. They're already waiting for you in the lobby."

"Of course they are. Evidently, punctuality isn't the cause of their separation," I mumbled.

"What's got you in such a foul mood this morning?" he asked, rifling through patient files. "I thought Mr. Sexy from the bar took you home last night."

Brad and I had been friends since I started working at St. Therese nearly six years earlier. He was a new RN in the behavioral health department, and I'd been hired as a marriage and family counselor straight out of my master's program from Northwestern. Being the new kids around the wing, we immediately clicked, and it didn't hurt that we shared similar tastes in men. He knew all my deepest secrets–well, all except for one. I didn't tell just anyone about that one–not even my mother. Scratch that, especially not my mother. Not even Parker or my therapist knew the entire story–and I intended to keep it that way–forever.

"Did you not get lucky after all?"

"Mmmm, something like that," I sighed, rolling my eyes. "I guess you could say that I'm going through a bit of a dry spell." He didn't need to know the exact length of said spell.

Coming around the other side of the counter, he leaned in to whisper in my ear. "Wait until you get a glimpse of Dr. Foster. That'll brighten your day."

"Dr. Foster? As in THE Dr. Carson Foster–renowned sex

therapist?" I nearly squeaked, my eyes widening.

"The one and only," a gruff voice answered from behind.

Turning on my heels, my jaw dropped as I took in the gorgeous man standing before me.

"Told you," I heard Brad mumble beside me.

I'd seen Dr. Foster once before when I was a grad student. I had attended a seminar that he'd presented on campus. He'd already been in the field for a few years and had come up with some revolutionary therapy techniques while he was an attending at Regional Hospital in the downtown area. I remember him being good looking back then, but the extra years had been good to the doctor.

His muscular arms filled out the white lab coat that he wore over a crisp, black dress shirt. I was almost certain that underneath it all, he most definitely had a six-pack. Dr. Foster clearly knew his way around a gym. Suddenly feeling insecure about myself, I wrapped my arms around my waist, making a mental note to try and hit the running trail after work.

Before I had time to contemplate any more of my own imperfections, my eyes came to focus on the cobalt blue tie knotted around Carson's wide neck, bringing out the blue flecks in his otherwise gray eyes. His thick, brown mane was styled with just a tiny bit of gel and a small trail of stubble outlined his chiseled jaw, leaving behind the sexiest five o'clock shadow.

Even the silver Rolex wrapped around his wrist was better than any porno I'd ever seen. Just because a man had never brought me to climax, didn't mean I couldn't enjoy the show. As I stood there gawking, I heard Dr. Foster break the silence.

"Dr. Carson Foster, but I presume you already knew that," he said. Offering me his hand to shake, I couldn't help but notice he wasn't wearing a wedding ring. I stood there in silence, forgetting how to speak. "And you are?"

"Ashlynn," Brad said, nudging me on the arm.

"Oh, yeah, sorry. I haven't had my coffee yet this morning. You'll have to forgive me. I'm Ashlynn Sommers." I said, hoping he'd buy my lack of caffeine for my sudden ineptness.

"It's nice to meet you, Ms. Sommers. I've heard so much about you," Carson replied, his eyes burning straight through mine. I thought about his words and wondered what exactly he'd heard about me–certainly, he wouldn't know that. After all, he was a doctor, not a mind reader.

"Only good things, I hope," I sputtered.

"Let's just say that Dr. Reynolds filled me in on all of the staff here," he said, his gravelly voice sending a shiver down my spine.

"Dr. Reynolds? I don't understand," I said, shaking my head. "Why would our boss be discussing us with you?"

"Well, she wanted to be the one to tell you herself, but she rushed out of here this morning before the sun was even up to head out West. I'll be taking over for her for the time being. She had an emergency with one of her elderly parents over the weekend, and she won't be returning to work for several weeks–could be a few months even. Fortunately, I was just down the road at Regional and available to step in for the time being."

This man was now my boss? This man, who in just five minutes had left me feeling more vulnerable than I'd ever felt around any man ever before, would be working by my side for an undetermined amount of time?

Noticing my sudden inability to form coherent sentences, Brad took control of the conversation. "We're lucky to have you here, Dr. Foster. You have quite the reputation in our field."

"I do take pride in my work. Now if you'll both excuse me, I have a patient to see," he said, turning to walk away. Before disappearing down the hall and into his office, he swiveled around. "Ashlynn, I should be free in about an hour if you're available to grab that coffee."

"Me?" I asked, pointing at myself.

"Yes, you. Dr. Reynolds did actually speak very highly of you, and I'd like to pick your brain about the department since it looks like I'll be heading it up for the foreseeable future," he explained.

"Oh, OK, sure. I'll meet you in the cafeteria in an hour then," I said nervously, as he disappeared into his office.

"Holy shit! You have a date with Dr. Sex." Brad screamed. "I'm not going to lie. I'm super jealous. That man is simply edible."

"Shhh. What if he can hear you?" I whispered. "Besides, it's not a date. And, Dr. Sex? What are we, fourteen?"

"Seriously, Ash, I've read articles about this guy. He leads the field when it comes to helping women who have intimacy issues. Evidently, he has a ninety-five percent success rate."

"Really? Ninety-five percent? I knew he was good, but I didn't know he was that good," I squawked, hoping he didn't notice my sudden curiosity.

"Yeah, why?" he asked, eyeing me quizzically.

"No reason. I've just had some patients with trouble in that arena, and it's not really my thing. You know I'm much more about communication."

"Well if you're so much into communication then you should have picked up the signs Dr. Sex was throwing your way. It's definitely a date. He couldn't take his eyes off you."

"You're so delusional. He was looking at both of us," I laughed, nervously.

"As much as I wish Dr. Sex swung for my team, he didn't so much as glance at my junk. He was far too busy ogling your goodies," Brad said, pointing toward my formfitting sweater.

Sighing, I pulled my arms around my midriff suddenly wishing I'd worn a baggier shirt.

"Would you stop it. You look gorgeous. You know how much

I hate those baggy sweaters of yours anyway," Brad said, reading my mind. "If it was up to me, I'd go to your house right now and burn every last one of them."

"I can't even with you right now," I chuckled. "Besides, I think I've left my clients alone long enough, I should probably get in there. Especially since I evidently have a date with Carson Foster in less than an hour."

"Yeah, you do! Get it, girl," Brad joked.

"Oh my god," I said, rolling my eyes before turning to walk away.

"Hey, Ash. How much do you love me?"

"A lot. Why?" I said, knowing he'd been hiding something from me.

"I may have forgotten to mention it, but there are a tall hazelnut mocha and cranberry orange muffin with your name on it in the nurse's lounge."

"Oh my god. You're the best friend in the whole wide world," I said. "Why didn't you lead with that though?"

"Well it was more fun watching you squirm and then Dr. Foster showed up and my brain went to mush with all that sexiness in the room," he laughed.

"You really are ridiculous," I laughed, sprinting off to the nurses' station to grab my fuel.

KNOWING I WOULDN'T be able to focus on my clients, I rescheduled their appointment feigning an emergency within the department. After all, it really wasn't a lie. Just thinking about spending time alone with Dr. Foster left my palms sweaty and my heart racing. This definitely qualified as an emergency.

With more than fifteen minutes to spare before our scheduled coffee meeting, I made my way down to the cafeteria. I was surprised to see Carson already standing by the counter with two cups of coffee in hand.

Standing in the doorway, I noticed him chatting with the cafeteria worker. Her eyes lit up and her smile widened with each word he spoke. Looks like Dr. Foster was a ladies' man. Unable to look away, I continued to watch from afar as they continued their mutual flirting. A new feeling crept up inside me, one which I could only explain as jealousy. I just couldn't make any sense of it. I didn't even know this man, and yet he was making me feel things that I hadn't felt in decades. Things that I'd avoided feeling all this time–even with Parker.

I'd made a terrible decision agreeing to come down here. Turning to leave, I heard Carson call out my name.

"Ashlynn, I'm over here," he said, just the sound of his voice leaving me on high alert.

"Oh, sorry," I replied, swiveling around and hoping he hadn't noticed me gawking just moments before. "I must've missed you. I thought maybe you'd gotten busy with a patient. I'd understand if you had to reschedule. In fact, maybe that's a better idea anyway. I have quite a bit of work to finish, and I hear the new boss can be quite the stickler," I laughed, hoping he wouldn't notice my unease.

"Don't be ridiculous. We're both here now, and I already have the coffee ready. Looks like there are cream and sugar over there. Let's go take a seat," he said, pointing to an empty booth in the corner. "And, just for the record, your boss isn't as bad as his reputation might suggest."

Sliding into the booth, my phone dinged with an incoming text. I stared at it for a moment not recognizing the number. Then it dawned on me. As much as I'd hoped to never hear from Jeff again, the text was a welcomed distraction.

UNKNOWN: *Hey, Ashlynn. I hope you don't mind, but I saw your phone on the table before I left your place this morning. I just had to get your number. I know we agreed on just one night, but after being with you, I knew I needed more. What do you say? Jeremy*

Jeremy! It wasn't Jeff or Jarrod. Close enough. Now that I knew his name, I had an even bigger problem to deal with. I really did have a clinger on my hands. I'd deal with that later but first, I needed to figure out how to make my escape from Dr. Foster.

"Husband?" Carson asked as I set my phone down on the table.

"No, definitely not my husband," I responded, not exactly sure why Dr. Foster had taken a sudden interest in my personal life. Everything was getting even more awkward between us, and I wasn't sure if I wanted it to stop or continue. After all, since he was taking over Dr. Reynolds' position, he was technically my boss.

"Not married then?"

"Not anymore," I admitted.

"Sorry to hear that. Care to talk about it?"

Definitely not with you, Doc. "Nope."

"All right then. Boyfriend?" he continued his line of questioning.

"No," I answered with a shrug.

"Oh OK, I'm sorry if I'm being intrusive. I guess it's just a habit with the job. The last thing I would want is to make you feel uncomfortable," he said, lightly grazing his fingers across the top of my hand.

"It's OK. I'm actually very single," I blurted out, suddenly embarrassed that I'd opened up in such a way. I definitely needed to get out of here.

"That's very interesting, Ms. Sommers. Very interesting," he said, smirking. "So, tell me about yourself. Are you from around here?"

"Me?" I questioned, hesitation in my voice. "I thought you didn't want to be intrusive."

"I'm sorry, I thought you said it was OK. And, here I thought things were just about to get interesting," he said, pulling his cell from his pocket. "Actually, I'm sorry to do this, but it looks like they need me back upstairs. Can we continue this later?"

"Sure," I nodded, as Carson excused himself from the booth. I sat there for a moment longer silently thanking the universe for the interruption. Little did Carson know, we wouldn't be finishing this conversation later. Not if I had anything to do with it.

three

ASHLYNN

S TEPPING INTO MY office, I dimmed the lights hoping it would relieve the mild tension headache pulsating between my eyes.

I'd become engrossed in a patient file when I heard a light rap on the door. Looking down at my watch, I was surprised to see that several hours had passed by. Assuming it was Brad, I yelled for him to come in.

"Yeah, I'm here. Come in."

"Sorry, I didn't mean to interrupt you. I just thought we could continue our little talk from earlier," a male voice responded.

"Oh, Dr. Foster! I didn't realize it was you," I said, looking up from my paperwork. "I just assumed it was Brad."

"If you're busy, I can come back," he said. "And, please, it's Carson."

Logic told me I should send him away, but I selfishly wanted him to stay.

"No, it's OK. I was about to call it a night anyway," I said, stretching my hand behind my back to rub out the knot that had formed at the base of my neck.

"Looks like you could use a little help over there."

If he only knew anything about my many problems. "I'm fine," I said, immediately regretting my answer.

"You sure? Some have said I'm a better masseur than a therapist. I'm not sure I'd agree with that assessment, but I do know how to use these hands," he said, his flirtatious behavior from earlier returning.

"Well, OK. On second thought, I guess I am a little tense. I've been reading over patient files all afternoon, and I must've forgotten to get up to stretch."

Closing the door behind him, he removed his lab coat and tossed it onto the couch. Stopping at the edge of my desk, he rolled up his shirt sleeves exposing the thick veins in his muscular arms.

"Fuck me," I mumbled under my breath. Even though I knew even Dr. Sex couldn't fix me, it didn't mean I wasn't willing to give it–and him–a try.

"I'm sorry. I didn't catch that," he said, apologetically.

"Nothing," I smiled, pulling my long, brunette hair over my shoulder.

"How's this?" Carson asked as he began rubbing my neck and shoulders.

"So good," I moaned.

"I understand you have another little problem," Carson whispered in my ear, his breath warm against my cheek. "Let me be the one to cure you."

"How–how do you know about that?" I asked, my voice shaking. "I haven't told anyone about that. Not even Brad."

"I just know these things, Ashlynn. I'm the best at what I do because I'm so intuitive to my patients' needs and wants. You're not the only one to refer to me as Dr. Sex, after all," he said, smirking.

"Oh god, you heard that?" I questioned, feeling warmth radiating across my face and over my chest. "I'm not interested in being your patient, Carson."

"Well, that's good because I have no interest in being your doctor. I have rules against that sort of thing. But, I knew from the moment I laid eyes on you that I needed you and I think you need me. Am I right, Ashlynn?"

"Mmmhmmm," I groaned, as Carson moved his palms from my shoulders slowly to my chest. He began palming my breasts through the thin cotton of my sweater. He'd barely touched me, and I already felt far more than I had before. He wasn't kidding when he said he was good with his hands.

"Touch me, Carson, please," I begged.

In a single swoop, Carson picked me up off the chair and sat me on my desk.

"Hands above your head," he said, his growing erection rubbing against my thigh. "We need to get you out of these clothes."

As he lifted the shirt over my head, I instinctively wrapped my arms around myself.

"No," he nearly growled. "In fact, let's remove this bra of yours. I want to see those perfect tits. I know they're just waiting for my lips." Dr. Foster was demanding, and although I pretended like I didn't–I rather liked it.

Unclasping my bra, my breasts sprang free leaving me bare to him. Cupping them in his palms, his thumbs gently grazing my nipples, he slowly kissed the side of my neck leaving a trail of kisses down my collarbone.

"God, you're even more beautiful than I imagined," he whispered in my ear, sending a shiver up my spine. Licking and lapping my breasts, he gently bit down on my nipple.

Squirming in anticipation of what was to come, Carson guided my thighs further apart with his roughened hands. Taking a finger under my skirt, he teased the outline of my thong.

Just as he began entering a finger into my pussy, there came a knock at the door.

"Shit," I squeaked, trying to put myself together. Looking down, I realized I was still sitting at my desk completely cov-ered–and alone.

"Come in," I said, trying to regain my composure.

"Hey, I wasn't sure if you'd still be here. I'm glad I caught you though. Monica and I are going to grab a drink to unwind if you want to come," Brad said, peeking his head around the corner.

"Nah, I think I'm just going to head home. I'm actually pretty tired," I said, my voice still shaky.

"You sure?" he asked again, opening the door wider. "You feeling all right? You look really flushed."

"Oh yeah, I'm fine. It's just a little warm in here, I guess."

"If you say so," he said, eyeing me with a smirk on his face.

"Trust me, I'm fine. You two go and have a good time. I promise, I'm on my way out shortly. I just have this one file left to go through."

"OK, raincheck."

"Of course. See you tomorrow."

"Same time, same place," he said, stepping toward the door. "Night."

"Oh, and Ash, I know you too well. You were just sitting at your desk fantasizing about the good doctor," Brad laughed.

What? I was not," I stammered.

"Don't even try to lie. You have sex written all over your rosy cheeks," he said, his eyes widening. "Unless he's in here right now."

"Shut up," I said, throwing my file at his face. "He's not in here!"

"So, you admit it then. You were dreaming about Dr. Sex. How was he?" he asked, a smug smile crossing his lips.

"Oh my god. I'm not having this conversation with you. Have a good night," I said, shaking my head.

"You ruin all the fun. Don't think I won't bring it up again tomorrow," he huffed, shutting the door behind him.

"That's what I'm afraid of," I sighed, shaking my head.

Standing to grab the papers that I'd thrown at Brad, there came another knock at the door.

"Let it go, Bradley," I said, as the door creaked open. He always got his panties in a bunch when I called him by his full name.

"Sorry to disappoint you, but I'm not Brad," Carson said, entering my office. "I was surprised to see your light still on. I thought I was the only one here still burning the midnight oil."

"No, I was just about to leave, but I got a little distracted."

"I can see that," he said, pointing toward the papers strewn about. "Everything OK in here?"

"Yeah, just Brad giving me his daily dose of grief," I replied, rolling my eyes.

"I see," Carson paused. "Is there something going on between you two?"

"Brad and me?" I laughed.

"Yes. Why is that so funny?"

"Well, it's funny because I think Brad would be more interested in you than he is in me."

"Oh," Carson chuckled. "I must admit, I'm a little embarrassed. I usually do a better job at picking up on the signs. Part of the job and all. Something must be distracting me today," he added, his eyes making contact with mine.

"It's understandable. I'm sure you've had a busy day. Being

thrown into Dr. Reynolds' cases as well as overseeing our crazy bunch," I chuckled, trying to lighten the mood between us.

"Yeah, I suppose that's all it is then. I could really use a drink to help unwind. Interested in grabbing a nightcap with me?"

As much as I wanted to say yes, I just didn't think it was a good idea. Dr. Foster had the ability to get me to tell him more about myself than I was willing to share. "Thank you for the invitation, but I think I need to head home. I'm pretty tired and Steve Urkel is probably getting hungry."

"Steve Urkel lives with you?" Carson snickered. "I thought he only existed in nineties sitcoms."

"He does," I said, flipping over a picture of my fur baby. "I picked up Steve Urkel at a local shelter a few years ago. We've been best friends ever since. Well as long as I keep him properly fed and watered. He gets irritable when he goes without his kitty kibble."

"Why the name?"

"Well, Steve Urkel is a bit of a klutz. He's always falling off the counters and knocking things onto the floor. I didn't quite know what to name him at first, but then I just pictured him saying 'did I do that?' and his name was born," I shrugged.

"I thought cats always landed on their feet though," Carson responded.

"Hmmmph, not Steve Urkel. He definitely missed that memo. Graceful he is not. I do love that little ball of fur, though."

"So, you're the crazy cat lady then, huh?"

"Well, I guess I'm a single divorcee who'd rather go home to her cat and eat a TV dinner than go out for a drink with an attractive man," I said, immediately regretting my choice of words.

"I don't know if I should be flattered or insulted," Carson laughed. "On one hand, I'm pretty sure you just called me attractive, but on the other hand you'd rather spend the evening with Steve Urkel."

"I didn't mean to insult you. I swear. After all, you are kind of my boss now. That'd be pretty stupid of me to insult my boss–even if you are here for just a short time. Besides, I can't really be the crazy cat lady. I only have one–at least for now," I laughed. "I have thought about getting a second one and naming him Fresh Prince though."

Carson just stared at me for a minute, not quite sure if I'd just told a joke.

"Man, tough crowd," I finally laughed.

Looking down at my phone, I realized another fifteen minutes had passed. I'd been so comfortable talking to Carson about my life that I'd completely lost track of the time. "I really do need to get going," I said, gathering my personal items off my desk.

"Let me at least walk you out?" Carson said, flipping off the lights as we exited my office.

"Sure, OK," I agreed, as he gently rested his hand on the small of my back.

CARSON

SINCE I COULDN'T convince Ashlynn to have a drink with me–even after a second attempt out in the parking ramp–I decided to return to the office to finish some paperwork. Even though I'd initially accepted this assignment on an interim basis, I was hoping my tenure at St. Therese would be a bit longer than I'd initially anticipated. I wanted to think it was the contribution I could make to the hospital that had me wanting to extend my stay, but deep down I knew it was the beautiful, brunette social worker with eyes of steel.

Never in my ten plus years in the field as a psychiatrist had I met someone as mysterious as Ashlynn Sommers and she wasn't even my patient. I typically had a knack for reading people after even the slightest introduction. It's one of the reasons that I was regarded as one of the best in the field of sex therapy. I knew what my clients needed and I knew how to help them achieve positive results. Some called me arrogant. I called it confidence.

But Ashlynn was different. I could tell from the moment we met that she was hiding something. Maybe because I knew a little something about that myself. Just when I thought she was opening up to me earlier in the day, she pulled away. And tonight, when I walked into her office, her alabaster cheeks were just slightly flushed–like she'd just finished an intense workout, or maybe something more. I wanted to ask her about it, but then again I didn't want to embarrass her and have her close off even more.

Staring off into the corner of the room, I considered putting a fresh coat of paint on the walls to better suit my taste. Maybe I really was ready to call St. Therese my permanent home. Just as I was about to call it a day, a stack of boxes caught my eye.

Opening the first box, I noticed they were old patient files that Dr. Reynolds had probably set aside for shredding. Just as I was shutting the box, one of the files caught my eye–*Ashlynn Flynn* written in red on the outside of the file. It couldn't be her. It was the universe's way of telling me that I needed to get this woman out of my mind. Surely Ashlynn was a more common name than I'd realized.

Flipping open the manila folder, I was stunned to see that it was Ashlynn's patient record. She'd been married to a Parker Flynn and the two had come to Dr. Reynolds about twelve years ago. She'd mentioned earlier in the day that she was no longer married, so I could only assume that they'd divorced and she'd returned to her maiden name. They probably sought counseling in a last-ditch attempt to save their marriage.

Glancing through the file, I knew I should stop reading. I was invading her privacy. Hearing a noise out in the hall, I quickly closed the file. Chuckling at myself, I wasn't sure what I was so nervous about. This was a patient record in my office. I had every right to be reading over it.

Reading Dr. Reynolds' notes on the couple, I learned that

they'd only finished one session of therapy. Joleen had concluded from their brief meeting that Ashlynn struggled with showing feelings of intimacy, but she wouldn't or couldn't disclose the reasons for her frigidity.

Finishing the outline of the session, I noticed Joleen had scribbled some additional notes in the margin.

The two had been childhood best friends who married shortly after graduating from high school. I could only assume that Parker had been Ashlynn's only lover up to that point. Maybe at her young age, she felt trapped and wanted a chance to explore other options. I don't anticipate these two keeping their follow-up appointment. Ashlynn seemed very adamant that she was through with continuing their therapy. As harsh as it sounds, I have little hope for these two.

Dr. Reynolds' words were harsh, but in this field, we needed to report candidly. I thought about messaging Joleen about this case. I was sure she'd remember it since Ashlynn now worked as a counselor at the hospital. I assumed she hadn't worked here at that time since there was no mention of it in the file. Besides, I'm sure Dr. Reynolds would have referred the case to another therapist since it would have been a conflict of interest.

I should have really taken those words to heart, but instead, I read through the file once again in hopes of catching something I may have missed before. Closing the file, I was discouraged that nothing more stuck out. I guess if I wanted to learn anything more about Ashlynn I was going to have to continue working the source herself. Flipping over the folder to place it back in the box, a phone number written in red ink caught my eye. Staring at it for a moment, I wondered if it had been the clue that I'd been seeking.

Deciding to go for it, I picked up the desk phone and quickly dialed the number. *"Hello, the voice mailbox you've reached is full. Please try your call again later."*

Slamming the phone down in frustration, I decided to call it a night. Hopefully tomorrow, I could learn a bit more about Ashlynn Sommers. I wasn't sure if it was the doctor in me or the man that had me so intrigued by this woman, but I was determined to find out.

♡

ASHLYNN

OPENING THE DOOR to my small, Cape Cod house, I nearly tripped over Steve Urkel as I walked inside.

"Hey buddy," I said, reaching down to pet my fur baby on the head. "Do you think they'll ever finish that construction at the end of the street? One of these days, I'm going to die from boredom waiting to turn down the road. And, we can't have that happening because then who would come and feed you?"

Meow.

"I agree," I laughed, walking toward the cat's food dishes. After putting down a fresh can of food, I opened the cupboards in hopes I still had at least a box of mac and cheese or can of ravioli hiding in there that I could eat for dinner. Fun fact about me, if there's one thing I hate more than cooking it's going to the grocery store. Oh, and I really hate washing dishes too. I blame my mother. She wasn't exactly Suzy Homemaker.

Sighing, when I realized even my secret stash of chocolate was gone, my phone rang from inside my purse.

"Hey, Bradley Cooper. What's up?

"You know you love me more than Bradley Cooper," Brad said.

"I do, but for the sake of honesty in our relationship, I'd rather fuck Bradley Cooper."

"Ditto, girl. Ditto," he laughed.

"I wouldn't expect anything less. Now is there a reason for

your call?"

"I was just calling to check up on you. I wanted to make sure you recovered from whatever I walked in on earlier."

"I told you before I was fine and to let it go. I was just about to head out to the store. Even my secret stash of chocolate is gone. And, after the day I've had, I desperately need some chocolate and probably a quart of ice cream too."

"I thought you said you were fine."

"Let it go, Brad!" I yelled.

"OK, OK, I give up," he agreed. "And, Ash, you do realize it's twenty-eighteen and you can order your groceries online and have them delivered right to your place, right?"

"That actually works?" I asked skeptically.

"Uh huh. Go put on your pajamas and order yourself some ice cream and chocolate."

"OK, I guess I'll give it a try. Thanks for saving the day."

"Anytime. Love you."

"Love you too," I said, ending the call before realizing that Brad never told me why he'd called in the first place.

Dialing his number, he picked up on the first ring.

"We just hung up. Did you butt dial me again?" Brad asked, answering the call.

"Hey, Bradley, do you think you could tell me why you called me in the first place? We got a little sidetracked talking about my lack of online shopping knowledge."

"Oh right. My sister said I could bring someone to my niece's birthday party this weekend. I'm pretty sure she wants me to bring a date to this soiree, but lord knows I'm not subjecting Everett to my family yet. He'll never ask me out on a third date, and we both know what happens on the third date."

"Oh, for the love of god, stop right there. I don't need the sordid details," I laughed.

"Whatever, just because you're a ho and never go on a second date," Brad joked.

His words stung, even though I knew he didn't mean any harm by them. "You know it's not like that," I nearly whispered.

"I'm sorry, Ash. I crossed the line. I didn't mean it."

"It's OK. I forgive you. But, I might just make you take Everett now after all."

"Oh, don't be a bitch. Please say you'll be my plus one."

"Yeah, I'll be your plus one," I replied.

"That's why you're my best bitch. Oh, and Ash, lace up your roller skates because it's at the skating rink," he said, ending the call before allowing me the chance to renege.

Ending the call for the second time, I opened the webpage for the local grocery store. My search, however, was interrupted by another incoming call. At this rate, I was never going to get my chocolate. Looking at the phone, I was even more surprised to see my ex-husband's name appear on the screen.

Even though Parker and I had divorced, we remained amicable. We'd been best friends growing up, and I'd always wished we'd just stayed that way. Parker pushed for a romantic relationship and at first, I thought it was what I wanted too. But everything changed in just an instant, and I knew I didn't want a relationship with anyone–especially with Parker. But since we'd always been inseparable, it seemed like the natural next step. No one at our high school was even surprised when we walked through the doors one morning holding hands. We married far too young–just shortly after high school graduation.

Everything on the outside seemed copacetic between us, but everything behind the closed bedroom door was so wrong. Initially, Parker thought it was just my hesitation because we weren't married, but it turned out to be so much more than that. Truthfully, it was all me, but I could never confide in him. We were doomed before we ever truly began. I mean, if you can't tell your best friend your darkest secrets then who can you tell?

In an attempt to save our marriage, I even briefly tried marriage counseling. I say briefly because I only made it to one session. The irony isn't lost on me because shortly after Parker and I divorced I decided to go back to school. I earned a degree in social work, and ultimately decided to become a marriage counselor myself. I figured that I would be well-suited to help women with similar problems. I might not be able to help myself, but I like to think that I've helped others along the way.

Parker moved on from me as well. He met a beautiful woman at his work, and they really are perfect together. The two are expecting their first baby in just a few months. I really couldn't be any happier for them.

"Hey Park," I said, answering the phone. "What's up? Is everything OK with Caroline? The baby?"

"Hey Ash," Parker replied. "Yeah, everything is good. I saw you called me from the hospital earlier, but you didn't leave a message."

"Nope. It wasn't me. I didn't call you today. Besides, I would've used my cell."

"Yeah, I thought that too, but I asked Caroline if she was expecting a call about an upcoming OB appointment, but it wasn't for her either. I just assumed it was you. Sorry then, it must've just been a wrong number. I guess we'll just talk later."

"Yeah, OK," I said, ending the call. Standing there for a moment, I wondered who would have called Parker from the hospital. A feeling of unease settled over me. Surely it couldn't have been Carson. Now I was just letting my imagination get the best of me. How would Carson even know about Parker? The topic of my ex-husband only came up briefly this afternoon, and I never mentioned his name. When he asked if I was married, I'd told him not anymore. And, that was the truth. That was all I felt he needed to know. It was all anyone ever needed to know. Because the more anyone learned about Parker, the more they'd learn about his brother.

five

ASHLYNN

FTER TOSSING AND turning for most of the night, I was up and at the coffee shop extra early. The previous day's events had me rattled, resulting in a restless night of sleep. I wasn't sure if it was Carson, or the phone call from Parker. Both conjured up ghosts from my past that I'd tried not to think about for a while. I was hoping with my schedule pretty tight, I could avoid Carson for most of the day. Glancing down at my watch, I assumed he was already making his morning rounds at the hospital, and maybe, I could sneak into my office unnoticed.

"Better make it a triple shot of espresso, Tina," I told my favorite barista. "I'm already riding shot-gun on the struggle bus this morning and it's not even eight yet. Oh, and throw in a strawberry scone. I'm wearing my sassy pants today."

"You know that stuff will kill you, right?" A familiar voice said from behind me. *So much for my plan of sneaking into the office.*

"Who says?" I laughed, turning to face Carson.

"Medical research," he said, seriousness in his tone.

"Last time I checked, you weren't a neurologist or an endocrinologist," I sassed. "And, shouldn't you already be at the hospital? I thought you doctors always did your rounds before the sun came up."

Rolling his eyes, Carson stepped up to the counter. "That seems like a pretty broad generalization. I prefer getting a full eight hours of beauty sleep. Besides, it takes me quite a bit of time in the morning to get myself looking this good," he chuckled as he turned and smiled. "I'll have what she's having," he added, placing a twenty on the counter.

"I thought you said that stuff will kill you?"

"It's a risk I'm willing to take," he said, handing me the cup of coffee.

"You didn't have to buy my breakfast," I said.

"Just accept the gesture, Ashlynn. I don't have any ulterior motives, I promise," he joked, raising his hands up in innocence.

"So, by taking this cup of coffee and scone, I'm not accepting a dinner invitation that I didn't even know was on the table?"

"That depends," he responded.

"Yeah? On what?" I asked, taking a sip of the hot brew.

"Are you saying you would accept a dinner invitation if it was on the table?" he questioned.

"I didn't say that at all," I laughed nervously. Feeling my heart rate jump, I wasn't sure if it was Carson's proximity to me or the triple shot of espresso jolting through my veins.

"You OK? You're flushed all of a sudden," he said, reaching for my wrist. "And, your pulse is racing."

"I'm fine. I probably just shouldn't have drunk that so quickly. I'll be all right," I said, trying to reassure him as the room began to spin around me. Even though it'd been years since I'd experienced a panic attack, I was almost certain that that's what happened.

With his hand still on mine, he tightened his grip. "Ashlynn, listen to me. You need to take a deep breath," he said, grabbing my coffee with his other hand before it crashed to the floor.

"I think we should take a seat," he said, pulling me to the corner.

Sitting in the chair that he'd pulled out, I put my head between my legs and began taking deep breaths.

Kneeling in front of me, Carson began rubbing my knees. "That's it. Just breathe," he said, reassuringly. Raising up my wrist once again, he measured my pulse against his watch. "That's better," he said, as I slowly lifted my head.

Meeting Carson's eyes, the look of concern written on his face took me by surprise. "I'm OK. I just need a glass of water," I requested between breaths. I wasn't sure if I really needed the water, or just a moment alone to gather my thoughts.

After just a matter of seconds, Carson was back with the water and the scone I'd already ordered. Taking a sip, I tried to stand. "Whoa, what are you doing?" he asked.

"Getting up. I need to get to work. I was supposed to be there fifteen minutes ago. I have patients waiting."

"The only way you're going to work is by going down to the emergency room for an evaluation," he said sternly.

"Carson, don't be ridiculous. I'm fine," I insisted. "I don't need to see a doctor. You were here with me the entire time."

"I'm not an emergency physician. I would feel much better if you had someone else look at you. We don't know what caused this. You could be dehydrated. Your blood pressure could be high. Your blood sugar could be low. It could be any number of things," he said, grabbing his phone from his back pocket.

"Please tell me you're not calling for an ambulance," I said, rolling my eyes.

"No, I'm messaging Brad so he can tell your assistant to cancel your appointments for the day. Should I call an ambulance?"

"Oh my god. NO! I was kidding. I'm fine," I yelled. "I only had a panic attack. I've had them before. I just haven't had one in a while. Now, will you get out of the way, so I can get to work?"

He looked at me once more before standing up. The look in his eyes telling me that my words had hurt him.

"OK, I'll go down to the ER if that'll make you happy," I sighed, reaching for my cup of coffee.

"I really don't think you should finish that," he advised.

"You're incorrigible," I huffed. "Can I at least have the scone?"

"Fine," he said, grabbing the bag as he led me out of the coffee shop.

"Since you won't let me call for an ambulance, I'm driving you to the hospital myself. I'm not taking no for an answer, so you can save your breath," he insisted. As we stepped outside, the cool autumn breeze was whipping the fallen leaves across the sidewalk. A sign that winter was lurking around the corner.

"What about my car?" I asked, pointing toward the green Chevy Malibu parked alongside the curb. "I'm not sure how much time is left on the meter and I'm out of change. The last thing I need is a parking ticket."

"Don't worry, I'll take care of it," he said, guiding me to the SUV, parked directly in front of my car. Opening the door for me, I slid into the passenger seat before watching him drop a few quarters into the meter behind us.

"That should do it," he said, sliding into the driver's seat. "I'll return on my lunch break and drive it back up to the hospital for you." Buckling his seatbelt, he checked the mirrors before pulling into traffic.

"You really don't have to do all this for me," I muttered as we drove down the street.

"I want to do it. We're colleagues now. I know I came across as a bit intrusive yesterday, and I apologize for that. I didn't mean for you to feel uncomfortable at all. It's just in my nature to ask the tough questions–even when it's none of my business."

"Don't even worry about it. I know you meant well," I said, gently reaching over to squeeze the top of his hand. "Thank you for talking me through that attack. I don't know what would've happened had I been alone."

"Shh. I'm glad I was there for you," he said, smiling. "Now let's get you inside and checked out. Wait here and I'll go get you a wheelchair," he added, pulling up to the emergency room entrance.

"Oh my god! You are NOT getting me a wheelchair, Carson! I'm perfectly capable of walking on my own two feet."

"Fine, but at least wait for me to come around and help you."

Not wanting to argue in the parking lot, I waited for Carson to escort me into the hospital. Finally, after completing the check-in process, and skipping the waiting room–perks of being a hospital employee–Carson agreed to get back to his work upstairs.

"Carson, thanks again–for everything," I said as the ER attending entered the examining room.

He nodded in my direction before responding, "Looks like you're in good hands here. Dr. Tyson and I graduated from med school together. Take good care of this one, Will. She's one of us," he added, patting Dr. Tyson on the back before exiting the room.

CARSON

NOT ABLE TO focus much on my work for most of the afternoon, I finally relented and called down to the ER to check on Ashlynn. Honestly, I didn't really want to leave her alone down there, but I didn't want to come across as crazy either. I couldn't explain it. I was her colleague–technically her boss even.

After poking through her case file and dialing the mysterious number, I'd decided to let it go. Whatever secrets Ashlynn was keeping would remain her secrets. But after running into her at the coffee shop, that intuition from the day before returned. Then when she suddenly got sick something else inside me took over entirely. I've only felt that way once before, and even then, it was an entirely different circumstance. I was a doctor. I was trained to handle those types of situations–to remain cool and collected in an emergency. But, I felt anything but calm when I saw her gasping for air.

Making the call downstairs, Will told me that he'd released Ashlynn just a few hours after she'd been admitted. She'd be fine. She was just suffering from exhaustion and mild dehydration which probably brought on the panic attack. He was breaking hospital policy by telling me about his patient, but since I was a fellow doctor at the same hospital he could bend the rules a bit.

Checking in with Brad, I learned that he drove Ashlynn home after insisting that she take the rest of the day off to get some rest.

Pulling up to her place, I noticed her car was back in the driveway. Brad mentioned taking care of it earlier. I wasn't sure if coming here was the right thing to do, but I had to see for myself that she was OK.

After opening her door, I could tell she was surprised to see me standing outside. Dressed in pink pajama bottoms and a matching tank top, she definitely wasn't expecting any company. Her hair was pulled back into a messy bun, a stray tendril swept across her rosy cheek. It took every last bit of willpower to refrain from reaching out to brush the hairs from her face. She was beautiful when she was pulled together at work, but this side of Ashlynn took my breath away. "Hey! I didn't expect to see you here," she laughed, pulling her arms across her chest.

"Sorry, I hope I'm not intruding. I just wanted to check on you. I called downstairs, but Will told me he'd already released you. Then I talked to Brad and he told me that he made you go home for the day. I'm glad you listened to him since it seems like you don't like listening to your boss."

"Yeah, you're both pretty relentless," she laughed.

"Well, I'm glad he did a better job than I did. How are you feeling?

"Pretty good. I took a long nap when I got home. I guess I haven't been getting enough sleep lately. It must've finally caught up to me. I'm sorry you had to witness my breaking point," she said. "Thanks for being there though. It's pretty scary going through that alone."

"I'm glad I was there just when you needed me. Is this something that happens a lot? The panic attacks, I mean?"

"Not lately. I haven't had one in years, actually. Not since I've been at the hospital. I thought those attacks were a thing of the past. At least until earlier today," I sighed. "I've just had a lot on my mind over the last few days."

"Want to talk about it?" I asked, hoping she might let me in.

"Nah, it's nothing I can't handle on my own. I've probably already said too much. If I don't be careful, you'll send me a bill," she laughed, nervously.

"You're not my patient, Ashlynn. I just want to be there for you–as a friend–if you need me."

"Really, I'll be fine. Besides, I'm sure you have enough to deal with from your patients. The last thing you need is for me to burden you with my problems," she added, turning her lips into a half smile.

"I'm always here if you need me," I said, giving her a reassuring smile.

"You know you could've just called. You didn't have to come

all the way over here to check on me."

"Well I didn't have your number," I shrugged.

"But you had my address?" she laughed, raising her brows.

"Something tells me you aren't going to accept lucky guess as an answer, huh?"

"Mmmm, probably not."

"OK, you caught me. I asked Brad for your address. If I'd just called, I wouldn't have been able to bring you this." I said, holding up a brown paper bag.

"If that's a bag filled with doughnuts then I need to call Brad right now and thank him for giving you my address."

"Darn it. He did warn me that I needed to bring you doughnuts for breakfast, but since it was dinnertime I went with a brownie instead."

"Brownies are definitely good too, but Brad is mistaken about doughnuts. They aren't just for breakfast," she said, with a hint of seriousness in her tone.

"Good to know," I laughed. "I also brought you some chicken noodle soup and crackers."

Letting out the most adorable laugh, "You know I'm not really sick, right?"

"I know, but I wasn't sure what else to bring you for dinner. A steak dinner seemed a bit much," I chuckled.

"I'm just teasing. Chicken noodle soup is perfect. Just what the doctor ordered," she said with a wink. "Oh my gosh. I'm being so rude making you stand out there in the cold for so long. Do you want to come in and join me? It looks like you brought enough for both of us."

"If that's really what you want. I just planned on dropping it off, but I'd love to stay for a bit," I said, hoping she believed I didn't have any ulterior motives.

"It's fine. Come in and make yourself at home. You might

have to share the couch with Steve Urkel though," she laughed, pointing toward the orange ball of fur sleeping on the sofa.

"I don't mind as long as he doesn't."

"I doubt he'll even notice. He's been out for a while. We spent much of the afternoon playing fetch. He's not used to me being home during the day–wore him right out."

"Steve Urkel plays fetch? Is he really a dog trapped in a cat's body?" I asked, truly impressed that the cat had actually learned to play fetch.

"Yeah, that's pretty much Steve Urkel in a nutshell," she laughed. "You two get acquainted while I change into something a little more presentable."

As I watched Ashlynn walk back to her bedroom, I had to ask myself once more what exactly I was doing here. No matter how many times I questioned it, I kept coming up with the same reasoning. There was something about this woman that I was drawn to–something so intense that I hadn't felt in a long time. I had a feeling that I needed Ashlynn Sommers as much as she needed me–even if she was reluctant to let me in.

six

ASHLYNN

TOSSING ON A pair of yoga pants and a Detroit Tigers hoodie, I stepped into the bathroom, taking a quick glance at myself in the mirror. My hair was the precise definition of a hot mess and the mascara which I'd applied earlier in the day now left a dark smudge underneath my right eye. Dampening a washcloth, I scrubbed my face before applying a fresh coat of light pink gloss to my lips. Rummaging through the drawer in hopes of finding a few stray bobby pins, I finally settled on two small rhinestone barrettes that I'd worn in my cousin's wedding to pull back the loose strands of hair.

Returning to the living room, I was surprised to see Carson had placed two bowls of soup along with spoons on the dining room table.

"Looks like Steve Urkel wouldn't share the sofa after all?" I joked, walking into the dining room.

"Nah, I just thought I'd get dinner on the table while you were changing. I hope you don't mind my taking the liberty of searching through your cupboards," he said, pulling out a chair for me.

"No, I don't mind at all. Thank you. Let me get us something to drink," I said, rising from the chair.

"No, no. Stay where you. Let me take care of it. Where are your glasses?"

"Second cupboard to the left of the stove," I said, as Carson took out a pitcher of purified water from the refrigerator and poured us two glasses.

"I hope it's OK, but I only have cheesy crackers for the soup. I forgot that most people just like plain, regular saltines in their soup."

"Of course, it's OK. It's like you read my mind. Cheesy crackers are best in chicken noodle soup. Actually, cheese anything is the best–especially cheesecake," I said, smiling.

"I sense someone has a bit of a sweet tooth," he said.

"You could say that," I giggled.

A moment of silence passed between us before Carson spoke again. "I didn't take you for a baseball fan," he said, pointing out my choice of wardrobe.

"Oh yeah, it's OK. I actually got this at a minor league game earlier this summer. The hospital pays for a suite for the staff to use during home games. Brad and I checked out a few games this summer. I'm still learning a lot about baseball, but the free beer was awesome," I laughed. "If you're still around next summer, you'll have to come to a game with us."

"I'd like that very much," he responded, shaking his head.

"What?" I asked. "You look confused about something. Was it something I said?"

"You just surprise me that's all. I didn't take you for a beer girl, either."

"Ha! Well, I don't drink a lot, but I can throw down a few

brewskies especially if they're free. Don't get too excited though, I like a glass of wine and a fruity cocktail too."

"Noted," he said with a smile.

"So, do you know how long you'll be at St. Therese?"

"Not exactly, probably at the very least through the end of the year. Looks like you'll have to put up with me for a few months anyway."

"Nah, I'd hardly call it 'putting up' with you," I said, reassuringly. "Actually, I have a feeling that I'll like having you around."

"I think I'll like being around, too," he said, giving me a half smile, which highlighted the dimples in his cheeks.

After clearing the dishes from the table, I realized I didn't want the night with Carson to end. I was actually enjoying his company and wasn't really feeling like being alone.

"Wow, a man who brings dinner and cleans up afterward," I remarked. "How are you single, Doctor Foster?"

"Sounds like a question my grandmother asks me every time I call her," he joked.

"And, he makes time for his grandma. You must obviously be a serial killer in your spare time," I said, laughing.

"No, nothing quite that serious. I date occasionally, but it's hard to find the time for a serious relationship with my schedule. I guess I'm married to my job and my other commitments–at least for now."

"Fair enough," I said, as Carson stood from his chair. I hoped I hadn't scared him away asking about his personal life. After all, a relationship was the furthest thing on my mind. "You weren't planning on eating and running?" I asked.

"Well, I should probably get going. I don't want to overstay my welcome, and you should probably get some more rest anyway," he said. Noticing the disappointment in my face, he quickly changed his tune, "Unless of course, you want me to stay?"

"I would like you to stay. I enjoy the company. I'm usually not very good with chit-chat, but you really do know how to make it easy. Besides, I believe you said something about brownies earlier?"

"Yes, how could I forget?" he said, grabbing the brownies from the paper bag he'd carried the soup in.

"Do you want to eat those in the living room? We can play a game of Scrabble, or watch a movie? Whatever you want to do."

"Scrabble sounds good to me. You play a lot?"

"Nah, I haven't played in years. My dad would play it with me whenever I was sick growing up. That's what made me think of it," I said, reminiscing back to the days when everything seemed easier.

An hour later, with the score tied at 300 points each, I looked down at my remaining letters. Using the board to my advantage, I gave Carson a sly smile as I went in for the kill.

"F-L-A-P-J-A-C-K," I spelled. "And, since I just used all my tiles and landed on a double letter score that's 84 points. Looks like I win!"

"Not so fast, Sommers," Carson said, returning with a sly smile of his own. "S-Q-U-E-E-Z-E," he spelled. "That's all my tiles as well as a TRIPLE letter score for the Z. That's 95 points for me. I think my 395 beats your 384."

"Wow, you're much better at this game than my dad. I always won when I was a kid," I laughed. Looking back on it, since my dad was an English teacher, he was more than likely letting me win all those times. I'd be sure to bring it up the next time I was over for Sunday dinner at my parents' place.

"I did graduate from Harvard Medical. I guess it got me something other than a piece of expensive paper that I hang on the office wall," he chuckled.

As Carson put away the Scrabble tiles, I searched for a movie on Netflix. Stopping on one of my favorites, *How to Lose a Guy in 10 Days*, I put the remote back on the coffee table. "I hope you don't mind if we watch a chick flick," I asked.

"Don't mind at all," he said, sitting on the couch beside me.

"So, was this the evening you had in mind when you mentioned the possibility of dinner being on the table? You know, before I had my meltdown on you earlier."

"Not exactly, but I think I preferred this much better. I really enjoyed everything about tonight," he said.

"Me too," I said, my eyes meeting his. Just when I thought Carson might come in for a kiss, he pulled away, leaving me breathless and wanting.

"Looks like the movie's starting," he said, turning to face the screen.

"Right," I muttered mostly to myself as I turned, hoping to hide my disappointment.

CARSON

AS MUCH AS I'd wanted to kiss Ashlynn, I knew the timing wasn't quite right. Although she'd opened up so much, I didn't want to risk scaring her away. Knowing I'd disappointed her, killed me inside. We sat in silence for the majority of the movie.

Shortly before the end, her head started to nod. I could tell she was getting tired and as much as I'd enjoyed spending the evening with her, I knew she needed to get her rest.

"Ash, I should probably get going so you can get some sleep," I whispered, as she rested her head against my shoulder.

"I'm fine. It's almost over anyway. Just stay until the end," she muttered as she drifted off to sleep.

As the credits began rolling, she began to lightly snore. She was adorable and although I wanted to stay with her like this all night, I knew I couldn't. Not wanting to wake her, I scooped her up into my arms and carried her to the bedroom. With Steve Urkel weaving between my feet, I laid Ashlynn on the mattress and covered her with the comforter which had been bunched up at the foot of the bed.

Placing a gentle kiss on her forehead, I turned and quietly walked toward the hallway.

"Carson," she mumbled, just as I began closing the bedroom door. "Thank you."

Not being sure if she was just talking in her sleep, I decided to leave her a quick note before leaving.

Ash,

I had a great time tonight. Thank you for the conversation and for letting me win at Scrabble. I hope we can do it again soon. Maybe next time you'll let me take you out for a real dinner. Enjoy your weekend. If you need anything, please call. I may have taken the liberty to leave my number in your cell phone. We'll see you Monday.

Sincerely,

Carson

Placing the note on her kitchen island, I flipped the lights off before locking the door and letting myself out.

seven

ASHLYNN

*W*AKING JUST BEFORE sunrise, I was surprised to find myself still dressed and in my own bed. The last thing I remembered was watching the movie with Carson and dozing off on the couch. Reaching for my phone, I wasn't even sure what day it was. I sighed in relief when Saturday appeared at the top.

"Steve Urkel, what happened last night?" I asked the cat who was sleeping between my feet at the end of the bed. "Oh, that's right, you can't talk. I should've taken a trick out of Sabrina's book and named you Salem Saberhagen and then maybe you could've answered me. On second thought, I think I like you quiet."

Meow.

"Yep, definitely like you better when you're quiet," I sassed, walking into the bathroom.

After washing my face and taking care of business, I padded to the kitchen to start a pot of coffee. Yes, I said pot. I still couldn't get behind those single-cup machines. Nope, this girl needed an entire pot to jump-start her day. Pulling a filter from the cupboard, I noticed a note from Carson left on the counter.

"Oh god, I hope I didn't mumble anything stupid, or drool on his shoulder," I said out loud.

Meow.

"You're no help," I accused Steve Urkel, chucking one of his toy mice across the room.

Meow.

"What do you want? Go get the damn mouse!"

Meow.

"Fine," I huffed, opening the cupboard and taking out a fresh can of cat food.

"I spend more money on your food than I do on my own. You do realize that, right?"

Plopping down the can of food, my phone rang beside me.

"Hello," I said without even looking to see who was calling.

"Hi Baby! Dad and I were wondering if you wanted to come over for lunch this afternoon? We haven't seen you in weeks. We miss you!" my mom said from the other end.

"Hi Mom, I wish I could, but I promised Brad I'd go to this roller-skating-party thing with him. It's his niece's birthday and I guess he needs me to act as a buffer between him and his sister."

As much as I loved my parents, I was glad I had an excuse not to go to lunch. Whenever I was with them, the topic of my divorce would always come up—no matter how many times I told them that I didn't want to discuss it. They'd always loved Parker. I think it had crushed them more when I asked for the separation than it did Parker.

"Roller-skating?" Mom asked, concern in her voice. "Are you sure that's something you should be doing at your age?"

"Thanks, Mom, I'm thirty-five. Not dead. I think I can handle a few laps around a roller rink. You know, I even started yoga last week," I lied, hoping she'd drop it. Truthfully, I wasn't really the most physically fit person. I did own a treadmill, but it served more as a clothes rack ninety-five percent of the time. It was a good thing with my work schedule that I didn't really have time to eat and I survived solely on coffee and protein bars–chocolate-flavored of course.

"Oh, I love yoga! We should go together sometime!" she insisted. Well shit, that backfired. I should've known my mother did yoga. When I was a child in the eighties, she was always the first one to buy the latest gimmicks in exercise gear. I think she was the second person behind Suzanne Somers to own a Thigh Master and she was the first to "sweat to the oldies" with Richard Simmons. Before she could ask any more questions about my daily exercise routine, we were interrupted by an incoming call from Brad.

"Gotta go, Mom. I have another call coming in–looks like it's someone from work," I said. *Don't judge, technically, it wasn't a lie.*

"OK, Baby, get back to me next week about the yoga and lunch. Love you. Oh, and Daddy said 'hi,'" she said.

"Love you and Dad, too. Bye, Mom," I said, switching over the call.

"Hey Brad, thanks for saving me," I said.

"You're welcome, I think," he chuckled.

"Mom was on the other line when you called. She wants me to go to yoga with her, but you buzzed in before I could respond. I already lied to her about going to yoga alone. I didn't really want to lie to her twice in the same conversation. I feel like there are unwritten rules about how many times a daughter can lie to her mother in one phone call."

"You're probably right about that," he responded. "You're still coming to the roller rink with me later? I wasn't sure you'd be feeling up to it after your little incident yesterday."

"Yeah, I'll be there. I'm actually feeling a lot better."

"That's good to hear. Hey, just so you know, I may have given Carson your address," he confessed.

"Yeah? Why would you have done that?" I asked, hiding from him that I already knew his secret.

"He mentioned wanting to send you delivery take-out. I didn't think you'd turn down free food."

"He did get me delivery. In fact, Carson delivered it right to my house last night," I told him.

"Shut your face! Doctor Sexy was actually at your house last night? Did he stay?"

"Yeah, we had dinner together."

"That's it? You know you can't leave me hanging like that. I need the dirt, Girlfriend!"

"We had a good time. He beat me at Scrabble and then we watched a movie. I fell asleep and he let himself out. That's it."

"Wait, he didn't let you win? He's competitive and delicious on the eyes. Doctor Sexy is just the gift that keeps on giving, isn't he?"

"You're ridiculous," I laughed.

"So, you didn't have wild passionate sex on the dining room table?"

"No, we didn't even kiss. He may have pecked me on the forehead after he carried me to bed, but I could have imagined all of it. I don't know. Honestly, it's all really confusing, and I'd rather not talk about it anymore."

"There you go again. Always shutting me out just when it's getting juicy," he pouted.

"I'm sorry. You know I just have a hard time talking about that kind of shit," I tried explaining. "Anyway, I should probably hop in the shower and get ready for the party. I'll meet you at the rink in an hour."

"Sounds good. Love you," he said.

"Love you too."

"Oh, and Ash, you know I'm not actually letting this go that easily, right?"

"I wouldn't expect anything else. Bye, Bradley," I said, ending the call.

♡

LACING UP MY skates, a familiar face caught the corner of my eye. Offering a friendly wave, I was surprised when Carson completely ignored the gesture. What the hell was he doing at the roller rink and why didn't he mention it when I'd told him my plans the night before. I was certain I'd told him that I'd be there. Before I had a chance to skate over to him, Brad skated in front of me, interrupting my thoughts.

"You ready to get this party started?" Brad asked, shaking his bootie. I couldn't help but laugh at his choice of clothing.

"You look like a unicorn just threw up a rainbow," I joked.

"Whatever, you just wish you looked this hot. No one can pull off glitter as well as I can," he said, doing a pirouette.

"The eighties called, and they want their leg warmers back."

"Did you forget we're at a roller rink? This is like an eighties nirvana," he quipped, as the best of John Travolta and Olivia Newton-John began playing over the loudspeaker.

"Of course, what was I thinking? I'm not sure what's brighter though, your shorts or the disco ball," I laughed, pointing toward the ceiling.

"Don't mock the disco ball. That would look awesome in my bedroom. Can you imagine getting lucky under that thing?

"You're so extra," I said, shaking my head. "I suppose you think I should've worn blue eyeshadow and put my hair in a Scrunchie?"

"Oh god, no. Those should've been banned thirty years ago,

Honey," he said like I'd just insulted his beloved decade.

"Where are your sister and the kids anyway? I thought this was a birthday party," I said, stepping slowly out onto the rink.

"They're on the way. She just called and said they were stopped in some construction. I went ahead and placed an order for some pizzas so it's all ready when the girls arrive. Oh, and I ordered a pitcher of margaritas for the grownups. God bless a skating rink with a bar."

"Uh huh, sounds good," I said, focusing on the blond woman and young boy who just appeared at Carson's side. I'd spent the entire evening with Carson and he'd never so much as mentioned a child or another woman.

"You all right in there? I just said pitcher of margaritas!" he screamed, shaking my shoulder.

"Yeah, I'm fine. Just still a little worn out, I guess. I'll be fine," I said, suddenly feeling nauseous. "You sure? You seem distracted today. Even more so than usual," Brad joked.

"Yeah, I said, I'm fine. I think your sisters and the kids just got here anyway," I said, pointing toward the skate rental counter, thankful for the distraction.

Taking a few laps around the rink, I tried not focusing all my energy on watching Carson playing with the young boy–the two laughing as he skated with him on his shoulders. Was it his son? His girlfriend's son? I'd spent so much time answering all his questions the previous night that I guess I'd failed to ask too many of my own. Not that, 'Do your girlfriend and son know you're spending the entire night at my place' would have come up in conversation. This is why I didn't let men in my life. They just ended up hurting me.

Somehow Brad hadn't noticed Carson, or if he had, he didn't mention it. And, Carson completely ignored us both as if he'd never seen us a day in his life. I knew it shouldn't, but it hurt. It fucking hurt—a lot.

"I think I'm going to get going," I said, as Brad circled past me for the hundredth time. I would never admit this to her, but my mother was right. The days of roller-skating were well past me. "I think I need to hit the gym for a year before I let you drag me back to this place," I added with a laugh.

"OK, go home and get some rest. I'll see you at work on Monday," he said, blowing me a kiss before his niece skated over, pulling him back into the middle of the rink.

Unlacing my skates, I looked back toward the table where Carson and his little surprise family had been sitting, only to see it empty. He'd left without saying a single word.

eight

ASHLYNN

"**R**EMIND ME AGAIN why I agreed to go out with you tonight?" I asked Brad as I sat in a dingy downtown Karaoke bar. I didn't come out this way often. I tried sticking near the west side of town, closer to my house and work when I went out. This was definitely outside my comfort zone. "And, why on Earth did you want to come here of all places?"

Even though the statewide smoking ban had been enacted nearly a decade ago, the walls of the bar still held onto the yellow hue from the smoke and the carpeting reeked of stale cigarettes. It was in need of a fresh coat of paint and a deep cleaning in the worst way.

"This place could definitely use a makeover," I said, taking a sip of gin and cranberry. "I'm pretty sure my grandma had that linoleum in her kitchen before I was even born," I added, pointing toward the floor covering behind the bar.

"And here I thought I was the prima donna, Judgy McJudgerston," he said, exasperatedly. "Sure, this might not be the most glamorous of places, but trust me when I say it's where you can find the hottest slice of man meat. Just you wait until you hear their silky voices. They'll have you itching to crawl into bed before they even finish the first verse."

"You know this isn't a gay bar, right?" I laughed, directing his attention to the group of men who'd been outwardly flirting with the women sitting at the bar across from us.

"Girlfriend, I've never had a problem finding a new boy toy here. Besides, I thought you could use a little fun yourself. Unless you and the good doctor are exclusive now?"

Brad had been fishing for answers about Carson and me for the last week. I didn't like divulging information about my personal life, but, truthfully, I wasn't actually sure where Carson and I stood. We had a great time at dinner the other night, but then he completely ignored me at the skating rink over the weekend. Not to mention, I had no idea who the blonde or the child were with him.

I'd spent the entire afternoon on Sunday trying to come up with a reasonable explanation, but nothing came to mind. I wanted to give Carson the benefit of the doubt, but it just didn't look good. I planned on talking with him about it at work, but I'd only seen him briefly before he was called away from the building on an emergency case. He hadn't returned to the office before Brad dragged me out.

"No, definitely not exclusive. We're hardly even speaking," I admitted.

"What happened? I thought things were full steam ahead with you two. I was already planning my Man of Honor outfit."

Shaking my head at my best friend, I responded. "I don't know. I guess he couldn't handle my crazy after all. He didn't even acknowledge me at the birthday party on Saturday."

"Wait. Doctor Sexy was at my niece's party? I never saw him. Why didn't you tell me? You know I would've marched right over there and given him a piece of my mind for ignoring you. My job be damned."

"I know you would have and that's why I didn't say anything. I can't risk losing my partner in crime at work. I can only imagine how boring my days would be," I laughed.

"That's my bestie always looking out for me even if she really is just looking out for herself," he singsonged.

"Don't be so dramatic," I chuckled.

"Shhhh," Brad said. "The first singer is about to come on."

Turning to face the stage, my mouth dropped as an attractive blond man hopped up onto the platform. His sculpted arms filled out the sleeves of his black V-neck and his thighs resembled tree trunks in his faded blue jeans. The cowboy boots he wore left me guessing that he was going to sing a smooth Chris Stapleton or Luke Bryan ballad.

"You weren't kidding," I whispered in Brad's ear just as the first beat of the song began. I was nothing but surprised that instead of the country tune I'd been expecting, AC/DC's "Highway to Hell" blared through the speakers. That I was shocked was putting it mildly when instead of a deep baritone, the shrill falsetto of my favorite childhood cartoon character came squawking through the microphone.

Turning toward Brad, we both broke into hysterics.

"Why does he sound like Donald Duck?" I gasped, trying to catch my breath. "I thought you said these guys would have me wanting to crawl into bed, not run to the bathroom to stop my bleeding ears!"

"I've never seen this guy here," Brad shouted over the loud quacking, tears streaming down his cheeks. "He's so bad!"

In an attempt to escape the screeching, I excused myself to the ladies' room. Powdering my nose, I was relieved when the noise stopped, and a familiar melody echoed through the restroom walls. Deciding to give these Karaoke singers another chance, I stepped back into the dimly lit room.

I hadn't caught a glimpse of the singer on stage, but his rendition of Maroon 5's "What Lovers Do" was everything I'd expected from the first performer. This new voice was strangely familiar too, but not from childhood cartoons. I knew I recognized it, but I couldn't quite put my finger on it.

Turning the corner, I looked over toward Brad who had turned in my direction with a gaping mouth. His eyes widening as I came into view, he pointed behind him toward the stage and mouthed the words "Doctor Sexy."

Convinced I'd misunderstood what he was trying to tell me, I glanced toward the platform, my eyes locking with a pair of familiar gray orbs. Continuing with the lyrics, Carson didn't break our gaze as he finished the song as if I were the only other person in the room. The room erupted in applause as he stepped off the stage, my only reminder that we weren't alone.

"I didn't expect to see you here," Carson whispered in my ear.

"I could say the same about you. Come here often, Doctor?" I asked, suddenly forgetting that I'd been mad at him.

"Just when I need to unwind. I've always enjoyed singing, and usually, I go unrecognized here these days anyway. I did my residency not too far from here. I haven't run into a colleague or patient here in ages," he explained.

"Yeah, honestly, this isn't really my type of place. Brad dragged me out of the office," I said, pointing toward Brad who was obviously gawking at our exchange. Carson waved in Brad's direction before turning his attention back on me.

"Do you want to get out of here?" he asked, surprising me

with his offer.

"I probably shouldn't just up and leave Brad. Besides, after the other day, I didn't think you really wanted anything to do with me."

Scrunching his face in confusion, "I'm sorry I don't quite understand. I thought we had a great time the other night. I'm sorry I haven't really followed up with you over the last few days but catching up on Joleen's caseload has me extra busy."

"I see. So busy that you had time to show off your moves with a beautiful woman and her son the other night at the skating rink. Or maybe it's your son. We've never discussed children before–and why would we."

Shaking his head in a sudden understanding, "Oh, I think I know what's happened here."

"You know what–never mind. On second thought, you really don't owe me any explanation. But, just for the record, you can dance as well as you sing. You really seem to be the perfect package, Doctor. Too bad it seems you like playing the field, and I'm not really interested in being the other woman," I said, turning to walk away.

Lightly grabbing my forearm, Carson stopped me before I could get out of his reach. "Trust me, Ashlynn, when I say I'm only currently interested in one woman. And, since I dance like I have two left feet, I can almost certainly guarantee that it was my twin brother, Camden, that you saw at the roller rink. Not me."

"Twin? You have a twin brother?" I asked, sheepishly. Even with all the possible scenarios I'd come up with the previous day, a twin brother had never come to mind.

"I do. And the woman he was with was probably his ex and their son, Sam."

"She didn't look like his ex," I muttered.

"They don't know what they are most days."

"I'm sorry. I didn't know you had a brother let alone a twin," I said.

"And how would you, if I never mentioned him?"

"Are you two not close?" I asked, hoping I wasn't prying.

"Yeah, we're both just really busy so we don't see each other often. He's actually a doctor, too–a pediatrician. He was actually traveling for a while with Doctors Without Borders. He hadn't called to tell me he was home though. Looks like I'll have to find out what that's all about."

"Oh, wow," I said, suddenly feeling guilty for ever doubting him. "Two doctors in the family, huh? Just a small difference between a sex therapist and a pediatrician though."

"Ha! We get that a lot. They're really quite similar when you think about it. If it weren't for me helping to make the babies, then he wouldn't have any patients to treat. My brother should really be thanking me," he chuckled.

"I'm sure he doesn't see it that way," I said, smiling.

"No, not so much. Anyway, now that we've cleared that up, I do need to apologize for just leaving the other night. I didn't want to wake you and I really didn't know what else to do."

"Oh, no need to apologize! I'm sorry for falling asleep. I didn't drool on you, did I?

"Nothing a washing machine couldn't take care of," he said, winking.

"Oh my god, I'm so embarrassed," I said, my hands covering my face.

"I'm just kidding. You can relax, knowing I left your place drool-free."

"Well that's a relief," I said as Brad walked toward us, his arm wrapped around a man who resembled a Ken doll.

"You ready to blow this popsicle stand? I'll drop you off before I head over to Nick's place."

Eying him suspiciously, I whispered into his ear. "What about Everett? I thought you two were getting close? I remember something about the talk of a 'third date.'"

"Nah, we decided to see other people. So, this is me, seeing other people," he shrugged. I could tell Brad seemed hurt by his admission, but this wasn't the place to discuss it in detail. I made a mental note to talk about it further at work the next day.

"I didn't mean to eavesdrop, but I can take Ashlynn home if it's more convenient," Carson offered.

"You OK with that, Ash?" Brad asked, looking between Carson and me.

"Sure, that'd be fine. You go and have a good time," I told Brad.

"OK, thanks! You're the best," he said, grabbing my shoulders and pecking me on both cheeks. "And, thanks, Carson," he added, reaching out to shake his hand.

"He sure is quite the character," Carson said as we watched the two men leaving the bar together.

"You don't even know the half of it," I chuckled.

"Have you eaten?" Carson asked, grabbing my jacket from the hook by the door.

"Not unless you count the gin and cranberry I drank earlier," I said with a shrug.

"We really do need to work on your diet," he scolded, shaking his head.

"Now I'm not sure if you sound more like my mother or my doctor."

"Ouch. Both equally as bad, I think. Let me take you to dinner to apologize. I know of a perfect twenty-four-hour diner and pizzeria just down the road."

"Yeah, OK," I agreed as Carson opened the door to the cool autumn breeze. "You know, I don't typically accept rides from strangers, but here I am getting into a car with you for a second time just a few days after meeting you. There must be something special about you, Doctor Foster."

Shaking his head, he laughed, "You're never going to let up on the whole 'Doctor Foster' thing, are you? And, for the record, I certainly hope there's something special about me because there's certainly something special about you, Ash."

"You didn't just say that," I laughed, sliding into his SUV.

"Unfortunately, I did," he chuckled.

nine

ASHLYNN

ENTERING THE DINER, my mouth watered from the sweet aroma coming from the buttery pancakes slathered in maple syrup along with a side breakfast sausage.

"I think I've died and gone to heaven," I said aloud, forgetting Carson was standing right next to me.

"What was that?" he laughed.

"This place. It just smells delicious. I'm starving," I smirked.

"Doesn't take much to please you, does it?" If only he understood the irony of his words.

"Not when food is involved," I laughed.

"And here I was thinking I needed to wine and dine you. Little did I know you would be content with a greasy spoon like this," he said as we took a seat at the counter.

"What are you calling a greasy spoon, Doc?" a gray-haired woman wearing a bright blue, waitress apron said as she handed us two menus.

"Sorry, Franny. You know I love this place," he said, taking the liberty to order us two coffees.

"Come here often?" I asked, perusing the oversized, grease-stained menu.

"Yeah, Franny and I go way back. Don't we, Franny?" he asked, adoration in his voice.

"If by way back, you mean thirty-seven years then yes, we go way back, Sugar," she said, smiling. "And, who is this lovely young lady you've brought in tonight?"

"Franny, this is Ashlynn Sommers. Ashlynn, this is Francis Riley. Franny and her husband, Joe, own this fancy establishment."

"Pleasure to meet you, Ashlynn. How do you know our Carson?"

"Oh, we just work together," I explained, hoping she didn't ask any further questions.

"Ah, I see," she said, nodding in understanding. I could tell that Franny and I would become fast friends if given the chance.

"So, you've known Carson since he was just a baby then, huh?" I asked, remembering that Carson was just a few years older than I.

"Not just a baby, Dear. I knew Carson when he was still in his mom's belly. She was a waitress here many, many moons ago. This guy and his brother practically grew up in this place. Always running around causing trouble–even breaking a saucer or two when they'd toss them around like frisbees," she said with a wink.

"You didn't!" I gasped.

"Oh, we did," he chuckled. "Don't worry though. Camden and I had to pay every cent back to Franny and Joe from our allowances. Mom made sure of it."

"The two even worked for Joe and me before they were hot-shot doctors making beaucoup bucks."

"You were a waiter here?" I chuckled.

"Yeah, in high school," he answered. "Why is that so funny?"

"I just can't picture you waiting tables, that's all," I explained with a shrug.

"Yeah, my brother and I both did what we had to do to help our mom out. Our dad was killed in a car accident when we were three. Obviously, I have very few memories of him," he said. "We lost our mom in the same way shortly after we both graduated from medical school."

As Carson shared these bits of his childhood, a sense of ease that I'd never felt before came over me. No one besides Parker had ever confided in me in such a way–or maybe I'd never given anyone else the opportunity.

"I'm so sorry to hear about your parents," I whispered, placing my hand on top of his–the first sign of actual affection I'd shown anyone in years.

"Thank you. It was hard growing up without a dad, but we did all right. Losing Mom was tough on us all, but Joe and Franny really stepped up and helped Cam and I both through it as best as they could," he said, smiling affectionately across the counter.

"Joe and I couldn't be any prouder of what both you and Camden have accomplished. Speaking of which, how is that brother of yours? He hasn't been around here in months. I bet that boy of his is growing like a weed."

"As far as I know, they're good. Truthfully, I haven't had much time to connect with him lately. The new position at St. Therese has me pretty busy. Next time I talk to him, I'll tell him to stop by."

"You be sure to do that," Franny said.

As the two continued to catch up, my stomach growled angrily, interrupting their conversation.

"Oh my god, I'm so sorry. I'm so embarrassed. I must be hungrier than I thought," I said, rubbing my belly.

"Nonsense! We're the ones rambling on like you didn't come in here for some of the best chili cheese fries in the metro area," she said.

"Sounds good," I said, my stomach growling again in anticipation of what was to come.

"You can also add two cheeseburgers onto that order, Franny," he said, handing her the menus.

"Make mine a double, please," I said with a grin.

"I like this girl, Carson. Any woman who isn't afraid to eat around a man is a keeper in my book," Franny said.

"I think you're right, Franny," he said, squeezing my thigh under the counter.

"How about I get you both a Joe Special instead," she suggested.

"Oh, I haven't had one of those in years. Sounds perfect to me," Carson replied.

"What may I ask is a Joe Special?"

"Trust me, you'll like it, but it's a surprise. At least that's what Joe and Franny have been telling their customers all these years. They won't give anyone the secret recipe," he explained, smiling across the counter at Franny.

"Don't go flashing those dimples at me, Sugar. It wasn't until after we were married and I signed a non-disclosure agreement that Joe trusted me with it," Franny laughed.

"Wow, whatever it is must be really delicious," I said.

"You better believe it. Anyway, enough chit-chat. Two specials and a chili cheese fry coming right up," Franny said, placing the order at the window.

CARSON

"THANKS FOR DINNER. I had a great time tonight," Ashlynn said, exiting the diner. "You two weren't kidding about the Joe

Special either. I could've eaten two more of those, but I didn't want to look like too much of a pig."

"Ha! I think your bottomless-pit-of-an-appetite is sexy," I said, flirtatiously. It wasn't my finest move, but it was too late to take it back now.

"I doubt you'll be saying that when I'm as big as a house," she joked.

"Stop it. You'll always be beautiful," I said, playfully swatting her on the arm. "I'm glad you enjoyed yourself though and that Franny didn't scare you off with her many crazy stories about me."

"She came pretty close with that one about the fake rat in front of the health inspector. They could've lost their license, you know!" she lectured.

"I swear to you that it was all Cam's idea! I felt horrible about it for an entire week afterward," I pleaded. "You believe me, right?"

"Well, since it seems like my girl, Franny, has forgiven you then so can I," she sassed.

"Phew, well then, now that we have that out of the way, I hope we can do dinner again sometime soon. Maybe even a movie or something?" I suggested, grinning when I noticed a piece of the apple strudel we'd shared on the corner of her lips.

"What? Do I have something in my teeth?" she asked.

"No, just a tiny piece of Franny's apple strudel, right there," I said, using my finger to lightly brush it from her lips.

"Thank you," she said, her eyes pleading with mine to kiss her. I knew this time I wouldn't be able to resist.

Without giving it a second thought, I pulled her into me, gently placing my lips on hers. Our kiss was slow at first, neither of us ready to play the aggressor. After several moments, I parted her lips with a flick of the tongue as our mouths began dancing together in perfect harmony. Feeling her fingers rake through my hair, I deepened the kiss until we were both left breathless and wanting for more.

Pulling away, I blinked slowly to make sure I hadn't been dreaming. I hadn't been with a woman in quite a few months, but that kiss was nothing like any kiss I'd had before. I couldn't speak as Ashlynn rested her head against the seat of the SUV.

"That was . . ."

"Incredible," she said, finishing the sentence for me.

Knowing I couldn't take her right there in the diner parking lot, I closed her door and slid behind the wheel. Hoping she wouldn't notice the bulge in my pants, I buckled my seatbelt before pulling out into traffic. The drive back to her place was quiet, both of us seemingly lost in our own thoughts.

"I would invite you in, but I know we both have to be to work early in the morning," she said.

"Yeah, you're probably right. I had a great time tonight," I said, giving her a quick peck on the forehead.

"Good night," she replied with a smile. "See you in the morning."

"See you in the morning," I said as she shut the door. I watched to make sure she got inside safely before heading back to my downtown apartment.

ASHLYNN

BARELY CLOSING AND locking the door behind me, I stripped off my clothes and headed toward the bedroom. After a quick glance around the room, I was pleased to see I'd taken the time to make the bed that morning. Shutting the bedroom door so Steve Urkel couldn't interrupt my playtime, I padded over to the lingerie chest. Reaching into the drawer, I pulled a slinky camisole over my head, barely covering my breasts which were heavy in anticipation.

Leaving my bottom bare, I pulled my vibrating rabbit from the drawer before falling into the center of the king-sized bed, the luxurious satin comforter cradling around me. Pulling up the hem of the camisole, I grazed my palms across my already hardened nipples. Pinching the taut peaks, my bottom squirmed in anticipation of what was to come. *This may finally be the night.*

I replayed Carson's kiss in my head, the way his lips crashed upon mine, the way his thick hair felt between my fingers. He was gentle yet intense. I could tell he was just as hungry for me as I'd been for him. That much was evident by his growing erection on our drive home. I hated sending him off to tend to things on his own, but I couldn't risk the situation escalating between us. I had a feeling that I wouldn't be able to fake things with Carson. He was much too intuitive. He'd be able to spot a fraud from a mile away. It was probably why he was interested in me in the first place.

Typically, I didn't care for kissing. I'd do it, but it felt far too intimate. I'd go through the motions without actually letting myself feel anything, even with Parker for most of our relationship. I suppose I was much like Julia Roberts in *Pretty Woman* minus the whole hooker thing. A kiss hadn't evoked emotions in me since Kyle first kissed me all those years ago and those weren't feelings that I ever wanted to experience again.

Ridding myself of memories of Kyle, I exhaled sharply before placing the vibrator between my breasts, dragging it down my torso before landing just above my slit. Checking my pussy for wetness, I slid a finger inside stopping to rub my clit. Working myself to the hilt, I plunged the rabbit into my aching core hoping to finally relieve myself of the tension that had been building for years.

Staring up at the ceiling, I fantasized about Carson using his hands on my body. His mouth sucking on my tits as his dick slammed into my pussy.

"You like it like that don't you, Pretty Girl. You like it dirty, huh?" a voice in my head said. A voice I'd blocked out for years. Without any hesitation, I yanked the rabbit from my pussy and tossed it across the room without even the slightest ripple of an orgasm. Sliding under the covers, I blanketed myself in the protection and cried myself to sleep. Tossing and turning for several hours, I dreamt of Carson holding me in his arms. Feeling safe and protected for the first time in years, I opened my eyes to find it wasn't Carson holding me at all. It was Kyle.

Jolting awake, trembling, and covered in sweat, I looked around the bedroom only to remember I was alone. "Oh, shit that felt so fucking real," I said aloud, blowing out a breath. "It wasn't real. You're OK. You're alone. You're safe. It wasn't real," I repeated to myself.

Glancing at the clock, I saw it was just after four in the morning. I hadn't had a nightmare like that in over a decade–not since I'd gone back to college to pursue my degree in social work. Counseling others who'd experienced similar situations had been my own form of therapy. It'd been my coping mechanism–a way to ease my pain and calm my fears.

In the brief time since I'd known Carson, my panic attacks and now my nightmares had returned after many years of dormancy. I could only speculate that he was bringing something out of me–something that I never thought I'd revisit again.

Not wanting to go back to sleep and fall into the rabbit hole of my dreams, I momentarily thought about calling Carson. Even though I'd only known him for a short time, just hearing his voice would have a calming effect on my nerves.

I quickly squashed that idea, knowing that he'd want me to talk about my nightmares. That was one thing about Carson, he certainly liked to talk–a lot. I suppose that was the therapist in him. But, the subject of my dreams was not something I wanted to discuss, especially not with Carson. I was falling for him. If we even stood a remote chance at something real, then he could never learn the truth. I didn't want him to see me as broken. I didn't want him doctoring me.

I could've called Brad, but I didn't want to ruin his romp in the hay with Nick. I didn't agree with his behavior, but lord knows I couldn't judge either. I'd taken home a stranger or two in hopes of forgetting my pain too.

Before deciding to give sleep another try, I heard the cat scratch on the other side of the door.

"Oh shit, I'm so sorry Steve Urkel. Mommy didn't mean to lock you out of the bedroom," I said, hopping out of bed and throwing on a pair of pajama bottoms. *Meow.*

"Please forgive me," I said as he immediately began brushing up against my bare legs. "Well you don't stay angry for long, do you?" I added as we both headed back to bed.

Waking up just before the alarm, I noticed I had an incoming text message.

CARSON: *I had a great time last night. I really do hope we can do it again soon. See you soon. ~C*

Not sure how to respond, I typed out a noncommitting reply.

ASHLYNN: *I had fun too. See you at work in a bit.*

As much as I wanted to go out with Carson again, I wasn't sure it was the best idea. Those old emotions which I thought I'd squashed years earlier were once again resurfacing. I wasn't exactly sure why, but I could only guess that it had something to do with my growing feelings for him.

ten

ASHLYNN

AFTER SEEING CLIENTS all morning, I was looking forward to catching up on some reading during my lunch break. Reading had always been an escape when things in my life became too difficult. I'd always loved to get lost in the pages of a book, even as a child, but my passion for it really began after everything happened with Kyle and only intensified when things started unraveling between Parker and me.

Just as I'd become engrossed in the romance novel I'd been reading, there came a light knock on the door.

"Come in," I yelled, hoping whoever it was would hurry. I only had thirty minutes left of my lunch break, and I'd finally reached the good part of the book.

"Here's today's mail, Ms. Sommers," the new temp who'd been filling in for my assistant said as she opened the door.

"Thank you. I'll take it over here," I said, reaching over the desk.

As she turned to leave, I began rifling through the letters and bills before coming across an office memo inviting me to the staff Halloween party. Not thinking twice about it, I tossed it into the wastebasket. In my six years at the hospital, I'd never attended the Halloween costume party and I didn't intend on breaking with tradition now. If I had it my way, I'd just sleep through the entire day and not wake up until the calendar flipped to November.

"Want to run down to the cafeteria with me?" Brad asked, barging into my office. "I didn't get much sleep last night and woke up too late to pack a lunch–if you get my drift."

"Drift taken and go get your own lunch. I'm kind of in the middle of something here," I quipped, closing the cover of my Kindle.

"Oh, don't get your panties all twisted. I knew you were on your lunch break. It's not like you were actually busy or something," he said, sitting on the edge of the desk.

"You know I have a perfectly acceptable couch three feet away? And, for your information, I was in the middle of a book when you so rudely interrupted."

"I'm not sitting on your couch for you to go all psychologist on me," he shrieked. "There aren't enough hours in a day for my shit."

"You're such a drama llama," I laughed.

"I'd ask to borrow your book when you're done, but I can't handle reading on one of those things. I still need to feel the pages of a book in my hands," he said.

"Oh, I have it in paperback too," I laughed.

"Perfect! Can I borrow it then?"

"Absolutely not! It's signed. Signed books aren't for reading. Their only job is to sit on my shelf and look pretty," I said, nodding my head.

"And, you call me extra," he chuckled.

"Was there a reason for your visit other than your inability to go down to the cafeteria on your own, Bradley?" I asked, snidely.

"Yeah, I need a date to the Halloween party. Everett and I were supposed to go as Popeye and Olive Oyl and clearly that's not happening now."

"Sorry, friend, you know I don't go to that thing. I haven't celebrated Halloween since I was fifteen. I don't plan on starting now," I explained. "What about Nick from the bar?"

"Oh dear god, no. Don't get me wrong, the sex was good, but he was a bit dry for me. The guy was a total snoozer."

"Well that's no good," I said, pouting my lips. "Sorry, you'll be short your Olive Oyl."

"Oh, no, I'm clearly dressing as Olive Oyl. I need my strong sailor man."

"I should've known," I laughed as there came another knock on the door.

"Ms. Sommers, sorry to interrupt, but there's a delivery here for you," the temp announced, handing me a large bouquet of red roses tipped in black.

"Oh, thank you," I said, as Brad took the large bouquet, placing it on my desk.

"Looks like someone has an admirer," Brad said, snagging the card from the arrangement before I even had the chance. "I wonder who it's from?" Brad questioned, beginning to read the card out loud.

Ash,

I've enjoyed spending every minute with you over the last few weeks. I can tell there's still so much you want to say, and I hope in time you'll be able to fully let me in. Let me take you there, Ashlynn. Also, please accept my invitation to the hospital's Haunted Halloween Extravaganza. I promise to have many tricks and treats in store for us.

Always, C.

"Seriously, could Doctor Carson get any dreamier? This guy's perfect, Ashlynn. What do you think he's hiding? Dead bodies in his closet? Four wives in his bed?" he said, handing me the note so I could read it for myself.

"No, I really don't think he's hiding anything from me. He's been really transparent this entire time."

"So, are you two in a relationship then?" he asked.

"No, I wouldn't say that. We haven't discussed it or anything, but you and I both know that I don't do relationships." I reminded him.

"But does he know that? Because I'm pretty sure Doctor C thinks you two are a couple."

"He does not," I argued.

"Yeah, whatever you say. At least tell me you're changing your mind about the party now. You better accept his invitation."

"No, I'm still not going," I said, shaking my head. "I'll just have to decline. He'll understand."

"What do you have to lose, Ash?" Brad questioned. "You obviously like the guy. I could tell the other night at the bar. You practically had googly eyes after you saw him up on stage. We've been best friends for six years and I've never seen you that interested in anyone before. And, from what I gathered in the note, he clearly adores you."

"I hear everything you're saying, I really do," I paused.

"I feel a 'but' coming on," Brad interrupted.

"But," I continued, glaring at him. "I'm just not ready. Just please trust what I'm saying and leave it alone."

"Uh uh, not this time. Ashlynn Renee Sommers, you need to pull your head out of your ass and smell the roses, girlfriend. Carson is kind, caring, and hot as fuck and as your best friend, I cannot in good conscious let you fuck this up!"

I stared at Brad for a moment, completely in shock from his

words. He'd always let me get away with it before. Just letting things die when I didn't want to talk about them.

"Look, I'm sorry, but it's the truth," he added, shrugging. "And, if you don't march your cute behind down the hall and tell him 'yes' right now then I'm going with him in your place! He can be my sailor man–Toot! Toot!"

"You wouldn't!" I laughed.

"Oh, honey, I would!"

"Fine, I'll go with him. But you better be there the whole time in case I need saving," I said, my eyes pleading with him.

"That's my girl. Also, look on the bright side. If you play your cards right, maybe Carson will let you go bobbing for his apple."

"Oh my god! Get out! I have to get back to work," I said, shoving him out the door.

After I'd seen the last of my couples for the day, I grabbed the note from the bouquet. Carson's words really were beautiful. And as much as I was scared of letting him in and the nightmares that could return, I wanted to give us a chance, too. Kyle may have taken parts of me that I'll never be able to get back, and I may have let him take Parker from me, but I wouldn't let him take this too–not Carson. Not this time.

Pulling my phone from the drawer, I typed Carson a quick text.

ASHLYNN: *Thank you for the flowers. They're beautiful.*

The moment I hit send I noticed the three dots, indicating a quick reply.

CARSON: *I'm glad you liked them. I've been waiting to hear from you all afternoon.*

ASHLYNN: *I'm sorry, I've been with clients all day. I finally got a minute to myself.*

CARSON: *No need to apologize. Just say you'll accept my invitation to the Halloween thing.*

ASHLYNN: *Well I've never gone to the hospital Halloween party before. I wasn't really planning on going this year either. Brad even tried convincing me to be the Popeye to his Olive Oyl and I turned him down.*

Even though I knew it was a little mean to string Carson along by not immediately accepting his invitation, I still laughed as I hit send.

CARSON: *Oh OK, I understand. Hopefully, we can get together some other time soon then.*

ASHLYNN: *Carson . . .*

CARSON: *Yeah?*

ASHLYNN: *I'd love to go to the Halloween costume ball with you. On one condition . . .*

CARSON: *Anything.*

ASHLYNN: *Our costumes have to be epic.*

CARSON: *I'll wear whatever costume you pick out for me.*

ASHLYNN: *You may regret saying that.*

CARSON: *As long as you're there with me then I'll regret nothing.*

ASHLYNN: *So Peter Pan and Wendy it is then. ;)*

CARSON: *I probably should've put a no tights clause in there, huh? You know I've heard those things can cause shrinkage.*

ASHLYNN: *Ha! We wouldn't want that then, would we? You can relax. I was only kidding. I'll try to come up with something that we can both agree on. Something that doesn't involve tights.*

CARSON: *Sounds good. I hate to cut this short, but I have some patients waiting to see me. We'll talk soon.*

ASHLYNN: *Sounds good, Doc. Talk to you later.*

eleven

CARSON

$\mathcal{W}$ALKING UP AND down the aisles of the Halloween store for the last thirty-five minutes, I was getting frustrated that I couldn't find the perfect fedora to complete my Ricky Ricardo costume. After coming to me with several ideas, Ashlynn and I had finally decided on dressing as Lucy and Ricky for the hospital's Halloween ball. As much as she acted like she wasn't looking forward to attending, I could tell she was excited to dress up as the famous couple.

Turning the corner, I was surprised to see my brother and nephew rummaging through the pumpkin carving kits.

"Well look what the cat dragged in. I heard you were back in town," I said, getting their attention.

Camden stood as Sam ran toward me with his arms extended for a hug. "Uncle Carson! I missed you," Sam said as I scooped him up into my arms.

"I missed you too, Buddy! Looks like you're getting ready to carve pumpkins," I commented, looking down at the patterns he held in his tiny little hands.

"Yep, Daddy said I could make a ghost punkin just like he made as a kid."

"I remember that pumpkin. I think I carved a vampire pumpkin that same year," I said, lost in a memory.

"You did," Camden said in agreement. "We carved them for a contest that Franny held at the diner. Of course, she couldn't pick between us. Since we had to split the prize, I didn't have enough to take Colleen Henderson to the movies. She ended up going with Tommy Bradford instead. I wouldn't forgive you for months."

"You got over it when you met Jade. Besides, Colleen and Tommy have been married for years. Last I heard, she was pregnant with their fifth kid. They were destined to be together. I'm sorry, Bro, but you never stood a chance with that one," I said, shrugging.

"Yeah, I guess you're right. Speaking of Franny, I wonder how she's doing. I haven't seen her or Joe in months. I really wish those two would've taken our offer to buy the diner so they could retire," Camden said, shaking his head.

"They'll never leave. It's basically their home. But, I did see them both just a few weeks ago. Franny told me to tell you hi," I explained.

"Daddy, can we go now?" Sam interrupted, two more Halloween toys in his hands. "I really want to go make punkins! Hey, Uncle Carson, want to come to make punkins with us?"

"I wish I could, Bud, but your Uncle Carson has a date tonight," I said, patting Sam on the head.

"A date?" he said, his eyes widening. "Is she pwetty?"

"Like father, like son, I see," I laughed, turning toward my brother.

"Seems so," he chortled. "Now are you going to answer the

boy's question?"

"Yes, she's very pretty, Sam. Breathtakingly beautiful, actually," I said, smiling at the two.

"I can't believe my brother is actually interested in something other than his job. I don't think I've seen you with a woman since Marissa," Cam said in a curious tone.

"Yeah, that was a long time ago. A lot has happened since then," I said, remembering the carefree days before I threw myself into being a doctor and a caregiver.

"Isn't that the truth," Cam said, patting Sam on the top of the head. "Speaking of work, I heard a rumor that you'd transferred to St. Therese?"

"Yeah, the head of the psychiatry department had a family emergency. They needed someone to step in for an extended period of time. I was told it could be several weeks to several months."

"Really? When we talked before I left, you'd said you were only interested in leaving Regional if you got in at the facility in Minneapolis. Something happen over there?" he asked.

"No, I just needed a change in scenery, that's all. Honestly, I didn't really give it too much thought. They called, and I accepted. Don't worry about me, they definitely made it worth my while. Besides, I'll still be able to go to Minneapolis if that opens up."

"Oh, I'm not worried. You've always been able to take care of yourself, Big Brother," he said, patting me on the shoulder. "Except for maybe on the football field in high school. Seems like I was the one doing the protecting."

"Um, I played quarterback and you were on the offensive line. Last time I checked, that was kind of your job," I said, rolling my eyes. "And, watch it with this 'Big Brother' talk."

"What? It's true!" he joked.

"By sixty-two seconds!"

"Still counts, doesn't it, Sam?"

"Yep," Sam said, suddenly interested in our conversation.

"That's not fair. You can't bring your kid into this!"

"Looks like I did!"

"I give up," I sighed in defeat.

"That was easier than I remember," Camden chortled.

"I don't have all night to argue with you about your dumb shit. I have a date, remember?"

"Oh yeah, so how long have you been seeing this girl?" he asked, changing the subject.

"A few weeks," I answered.

"Have you told her about Marissa?" he asked.

"No, I didn't think she was ready for that quite yet," I responded.

"You ever going to tell her?" he pried.

"Eventually. She just has a lot of her own struggles. I didn't want to burden her with mine."

"If you say so, Brother. I just know you could use the extra support, that's all. I'm sorry I didn't let you know I was back in town. I've been meaning to call it's just that things have been complicated."

"Yeah, I heard you and Jade were back together. What is this? The seventh time?"

"How'd you hear?"

"My girlfriend, err friend, Ashlynn," I said, shaking my head. "Anyway, she saw you all at the roller rink a few weeks back. She thought it was me ignoring her the entire time. It didn't go over so well. I'm sure you can imagine."

"Yikes. Sorry about that, Bro. We haven't had to play the ol' dating switcheroo since college," he laughed, remembering the good old days.

"Yeah, we definitely tricked a girl or two," I laughed. "Anyway,

I should probably get going. I have to go get ready for tonight. I'm glad I ran into you two. Text me, we'll have to try and grab lunch one of these days to catch up."

"Sounds good, Man," he said, giving me a fist bump.

"Bye, Sam," I said, waving at my nephew.

"Bye, Uncle Carson. Love you!"

"Love you, too, Buddy," I said, as they grabbed their merchandise and headed toward the checkout lane.

♡

ASHLYNN

"I'M REALLY GLAD you talked me into coming to the party," I told Brad as we stepped up to the bar.

"Just say it with me. Brad, you're always right. Oh, and you have perfect hair, an amazing body, and impeccable fashion sense," he said, striking a pose.

"Yeah, I'm not saying any of that. Your ego is already bigger than my derrière. But since you're fishing for a compliment, your costume is marvelous."

"Isn't it fantastic? These tights really accentuate my bulge," he said, proudly showing off his junk. "The new nurse from the ICU keeps staring at me. Do you think he's into me?"

"Oh, he's pretty cute," I said, turning to look.

"Don't look!" Brad whisper-yelled.

"How am I supposed to tell if he's into you if I can't look at him?" I asked, slowing blinking at my best friend.

"OK, fine, but don't get caught!"

"Have I ever mentioned that you're ridiculous? 'Cause you are!"

"Yes, once or twice," he chuckled.

Just as I was about to take another look at Brad's new

infatuation, Carson came up behind us. "What's so interesting over here?" he asked, placing his hand on the small of my back.

"Bradley Cooper over here has the hots for the new nurse over there," I said, pointing so Carson could check him out. "He can't tell if he's into him or not."

"Oh my god! You'd make a terrible undercover cop with your staring and pointing!"

"Good thing I'm not an undercover cop then," I chuckled.

"Why don't you just go over there and ask him?" Carson suggested, turning to the bartender to order a whiskey sour.

"Carson, I understand you're technically my boss, so I mean this with the utmost respect, but you're just as crazy as your girlfriend here!"

My eyes widened, and I nearly choked on the soda I'd been drinking. "Bartender! Can I please get a shot of vodka!" I yelled across the bar.

Noticing my sudden unease, Carson quickly diverted the conversation from Brad's recent remark. "Hey Brad, I think the organizers need you over by the kitchen. I heard them say something about needing an emcee for the costume contest and your name came up."

"Well, why didn't you say something sooner?" Brad asked. "You OK over here, Ash?"

"I'll take care of her, I promise," Carson said as Brad looked in my direction.

"I'm fine. Go be brilliant."

"Oh, I plan on it!" he said, running toward the makeshift stage.

twelve

CARSON

WE STOOD ALONE for a moment, neither of us saying a word. I wasn't quite expecting Ashlynn's reaction when Brad broached our relationship status. It was a conversation that I wanted to have, especially after the kiss we'd shared, but I hadn't found the right time over the last few weeks.

We'd both been busy with casework, and the short moments we'd had alone, we'd been planning our costumes. On more than one occasion, I'd wanted to pull her into the staff lounge and have my way with her, but I knew that was far from appropriate behavior. And, given her recent reaction, she would drift farther away from me than ever before.

"Have I told you yet that you're the prettiest Lucille Ball that I've ever laid eyes on?" I whispered into her ear, tucking a strand of brunette hair under the bright red wig. With just the simplest gesture, she seemed to relax. Brad's comment was suddenly forgotten–at least for now.

"Thank you," she murmured. "You're pretty sexy yourself, Mr. Ricardo."

"Lucy, you got some 'splainin' to do!" I laughed, pulling her in closer.

"I think you're enjoying this too much," she giggled, music to my ears.

"I'm just trying to remain in character at all times. We're going to win this costume contest."

"You know it's just some stupid traveling trophy, right?"

"Yeah, but it's an awesome trophy that I plan to proudly display on the bookshelf in my office once we win," I exclaimed, exuberantly. "Do they engrave our names on it too?"

"Oh my god. It isn't the Stanley Cup!" she protested. "Have you been drinking Brad's Kool-Aid? You're starting to act like him and quite honestly it's scaring me!" She was really taking me seriously. I was all in now.

"What? Oh no! You haven't touched it prematurely, have you? You know if you've already touched it then we won't win."

"Like I said, it's NOT the Stanley Cup!"

"These are all acceptable questions, Ashlynn!" I said. "I wish you were taking this as seriously as I am," I added, bursting into a fit of laughter.

"Oh my god, you're such a prick," she squealed, smacking me on the bicep. "I totally thought you were being serious."

"Well, I mean it'd be nice to win, but I'm not going to lose any sleep over it, if we don't."

"You two are going to have to settle for second place," Brad singsonged, waltzing past us. "I've got this one in the bag. Turns out the ladies on the hospital women's auxiliary board really love a man in tights."

"I told you we should've been Peter Pan and Wendy," Ashlynn

protested, now suddenly interested in the victory.

"Nah, Brad really pulls off Lycra much better than I ever could. You watch, I'll go sway those ladies. They won't be able to resist my Ricky Ricardo accent. I knew there was a reason I'd been practicing for days," I said, smiling as I turned to walk away.

"Be sure to flash them those dimples while you're over there," she shouted.

"Oh, Lucy, you play dirty and I like it!"

"Damn, he's right. You're totally going to win this. There's no way those ladies are going to be able to resist that killer smile," I heard Brad tell Ashlynn. Stopping just out of their view, I listened to the remainder of their conversation. Maybe it wasn't right to eavesdrop on their discussion, but I had to get into Ashlynn's head. I had to know that my feelings for her weren't for nothing.

"Yeah, he is pretty irresistible, isn't he?" she sighed.

"Girl, you've got it bad. Don't you think it's about time you told him? Don't think I didn't notice your crazy eyes come out when I referred to you as his girlfriend earlier," Brad reminded her.

"I can't, Brad. I've thought about it a lot over the last few weeks and I just can't fake it around him," she sighed. Fake it? What did she mean by faking it? I leaned in closer, hoping Brad would ask the questions that I should be asking myself.

"But, you just said he was irresistible. I don't understand what you'd be faking, Ash. You're just as into him as he's into you. Help me understand."

"It doesn't matter. All that matters is, in the end, we'd both end up hurt. It's just easier this way. Trust me, I've been down this road before with Parker. It would have been easier if I'd just left him when he wanted more. I didn't have more to give then, and I don't have more to give now. It's just that simple," she said, tears spilling down her cheeks.

Watching as she cried, I should've run over to console her, but instead, I left the comforting to Brad. In the end, maybe Ashlynn was right. Maybe we would both end up hurt. Lord knows, it's a road I'd been down before and it'd taken me a long time to recover, but it was a risk I knew I was willing to take–especially for her.

ASHLYNN

"SEEMS LIKE CARSON has been gone a long time," I said, drying the tears from the corners of my eyes. Even though I knew things would never work out romantically between the two of us, it didn't mean that I didn't care about him. He'd been good to me over the last several weeks, and even I couldn't deny that the kiss we shared didn't have me second-guessing everything.

"Yeah, we should probably go save him from the flock of hungry women," Brad laughed, pointing toward the corner where Carson was standing in the middle of a circle of ladies from the auxiliary.

"I think he's motioning for me to come rescue him," I laughed.

"On second thought, I'm sure he's fine. It's good for him. I'm sure they could even teach the old Doc a thing or two. Who knows, it could even help him down the road with his techniques," Brad joked.

"Really? You two couldn't come over there and offer me some assistance," Carson guffawed as he rejoined us. "I thought those ladies were going to eat me alive."

"Looks like you managed," I laughed, as Brad was called to the stage to announce the contest winners. "Now that he's gone, were you able to sway them?"

"Oh, we're a shoo-in," he confirmed.

"Ladies and gentlemen, may I have your attention," Brad said from the stage. "In my hands are the results for this year's costume contest," he added, the crowd erupting in applause. This being my first experience at the Halloween Ball, I really was shocked to see how seriously the staff took this little competition.

After announcing the second and third place winners, Brad looked toward the crowd and gave me a knowing glance. We'd be happy for one another no matter who captured the trophy. "Without further ado, the winners of this year's Halloween Ball Costume Contest are . . ." he paused, opening the envelope. "It's a tie," he continued, shock in his voice.

"Who won?" someone yelled from the crowd.

"The winners are Ashlynn Sommers and Carson Foster and Lucille Ball and Ricky Ricardo and myself as Peter Pan," Brad squealed, hoisting the trophy over his head as Carson and I walked onto the stage.

"I don't think we'll ever be able to pry that trophy out of his hands," I sighed, shaking my head.

"I'm so shocked by this win!" Brad gushed into the microphone. "I'd like to thank the Academy, my coworkers, and my B-F-F Ashlynn, for without you, this win wouldn't have been possible. "

"OK, I think that's enough, Brad," I said, dragging him off the stage before he said something that would embarrass himself or maybe me. "Why don't you go show off that trophy to our colleagues?" I suggested, knowing I needed some alone time with Carson.

"May I have this dance, Lucy?" Carson asked in his best Ricky accent.

"Well aren't you charming," I said, grabbing for his outstretched hand.

Carson pulled me tightly against his chest as *Demons* by Imagine Dragons played through the speakers. I couldn't help but realize the irony of the moment.

"Hey, you OK?" Carson asked as we swayed together to the music.

"Yeah, it's just been a long night, that's all. I guess I'm just kind of tired," I lied, biting my lip to hold back another round of tears. I hadn't gone out on Halloween in twenty years. Even when Parker and I were married, I'd usually stay at work late just so I wouldn't be forced to go out. The other times, I'd come home, turn off the lights, and fall asleep before nightfall just so my memories of that fateful night wouldn't torment me.

"So, I probably shouldn't admit this, but I happened to overhear part of your conversation with Brad earlier and something you said has been bothering me," he admitted.

"Yeah?" I responded, preparing for what was coming next.

"You told him that you couldn't fake it with me. What did you mean by that?" he questioned.

Knowing that I couldn't tell him anymore lies, I tried my best to give him the most honest answer that I could possibly come up with.

"Look, Carson. I like you. I really do, but I can't give you more. I can't give you the relationship that I think you're looking for," I told him, my own heart shattering with each word I spoke. "I can't pretend that we'd make a happy couple when I know that we wouldn't. Trust me when I tell you that it's definitely nothing that you've done, it's all me."

"Sounds like an excuse to me. I know you feel as much for me as I do for you. This isn't fake, Ashlynn. It's very real. Trust me, you can't fake this. I won't let you fake this."

"There's just so much you don't know, Carson. You can never know."

"Why not?"

"Because I'm afraid I want more with you, and I just can't

have more," I admitted, a steady stream of tears now running down my cheeks.

"Then that's exactly why you should let me in. Let me give you more. Fight for it–fight for us. At least for the chance at something more," he begged, leading us into a corner where we sat, away from prying eyes.

"I'm sorry. I just can't. Please understand, Carson. I can't have more. Not with you. Not with anyone," I cried.

"Ashlynn, I've heard a lot of excuses from patients over the years, but I'm not sure I can understand this one," he thundered, pain evident in his eyes.

"You just can't ever learn the truth, Carson. I can't give you what you want, and I don't want to hurt you. I can't hurt you like I hurt Parker. I just can't hurt someone else that I care about."

"Then that's exactly why you should tell me, Ash," Carson whispered, kneeling in front of me, placing his palm across my cheek.

"Can you just please take me home? I think I'm going to be sick," I said, rubbing my hands across my face. "I knew I shouldn't even have agreed to come here with you tonight. Nothing good ever happens on this fucking holiday."

I could tell Carson wanted to continue our discussion, but luckily for me Brad came over to us, interrupting our conversation.

"Ash, I think I'm going to call for an Uber to take me home. I sucked down one too many congratulatory, caramel apple martinis and my head is spinning," he said, practically tripping over his own feet. "You going to be OK?"

"Yeah, I'll be fine. Carson was just about to take me home," I said, looking back in his direction. The look on his face was one that would haunt me for quite some time. The smile that he'd worn earlier was replaced with a blank stare, void of all emotion. He'd given up. Just like I'd asked him to–why did that hurt so fucking much?

"She's right. We were just about to take off. I can give you a ride too," Carson told Brad.

"Are you sure? I don't want to intrude on your alone time," Brad said.

"You're definitely not," Carson insisted, not even looking at me. "Let's go."

thirteen

ASHLYNN

BRAD'S SHRILL, DRUNKEN yapping about a community theater award he'd won for his portrayal of Frankie Valli in "Jersey Boys" was much preferred to the deafening silence of the drive after dropping Brad off at his house. Pulling in my driveway, I turned to face Carson who stoically peered ahead, not even looking in my direction.

"Carson, please understand. It's not my intention to hurt you. It's just for the best. Please say you understand?" I nearly begged, grabbing his arm.

Wincing, as though my hand was molten lava, I pulled it away, not wanting to cause him any more pain.

"I don't understand. I thought we were both on the same page, but it turns out we're miles apart. You won't trust me with your secrets. And, if I haven't earned your trust then what's the fucking point, Ashlynn? he barked, pain evident in his voice. His words hurt, but he was at least partially right.

"It's not like that. I do trust you!" I cried, praying he'd eventually forgive me. I didn't want to lose him entirely. I enjoyed the friendship that we'd built over the last several weeks.

"Maybe, but not enough. Listen, I think we've said all that needs to be said. I don't want to say something that I may regret, and it's not like we can just disappear from each other's lives–at least until Dr. Reynolds comes back. So, let's just go back to being colleagues. Nothing more. It's my fault for ever thinking there could be something more."

Seeing the torment in his eyes and knowing that I'd been the reason for his pain, had me on the brink of unburying my secrets.

"Carson, I . . ." I paused.

"Don't, Ashlyn," he interrupted. "You said earlier that you weren't interested in pursuing a relationship, so I give up. As much as I wanted to give you a hundred percent, I can't do that when I only get fifty percent of you in return. Now, have a good night. I'll see you on Monday."

Not knowing how to respond, I opened the passenger door in defeat.

"OK, then. Goodnight, I guess," I mumbled, stepping out of the SUV.

Before I'd even reached the front porch, Carson had pulled away, leaving behind only a lingering trail of dust.

Quickly changing out of my Lucy costume, I hopped into bed without even bothering to wash the layers of makeup off my face. I'm sure I'd pay for it in about fifteen years, but right now I didn't care. My only concern was making it through the rest of the night unscathed–fucking Halloween.

Turning on the television, I flipped through the channels seeing only horror flicks being aired, one after another. Turning off the screen, I hoped it wasn't a forewarning of the nightmares that were yet to come. As I drifted off to sleep, I was momentarily startled awake when Steve Urkel jumped on the bed, cuddling up to my side.

"Are you sure your mom and dad won't care if I spend the night?" I asked Parker for the hundredth time.

"No, Mom already said it was fine. They're going to a Halloween party with your parents, but they should be home later. Vanessa will be out with her friends and Mom said that Kyle would be staying at the house if we need anything," Parker said, reassuring me.

"OK, I just don't want to get into trouble."

"Seriously, Ash. You worry too much!"

"Sorry," I said, sticking out my bottom lip.

"You're cute," he said, smiling.

"Parker Flynn, do you like me? Do you want to kiss me?" I teased.

"What if I said yes? Would you let me kiss you?" he asked, catching me off guard. Parker and I had been best friends for longer than I could remember. Did I want him to kiss me? What if I hated it? Would we still be best friends? But, what if I liked it? I was fifteen and I'd never kissed a boy before. It would be nice to finally have a boyfriend to brag about to my girlfriends.

"Stop it! You're not being serious," I laughed, not knowing how else to respond.

"I'm being completely serious, Ash. I've wanted to kiss you for a long time now, but I never knew if you felt the same way," he explained, stepping toward me. "Do you feel the same way? Can I kiss you, Ashlynn?"

"Sure," I hesitated. "I mean, yes. I'd like it if you kissed me."

I don't remember it being an earth-shattering first kiss. I didn't see stars or fireworks, but I'm sure as far as first kisses go it was at least average. At least we didn't get our braces stuck together like Brett and Sarah, or he didn't slobber on me like Drooling David. I knew I liked Parker well enough, and I knew he'd be a good boyfriend. It seemed like the obvious choice at the time.

"So, you're my girlfriend now?" he asked, setting a large bowl of

popcorn on the coffee table.

"Yeah, I guess," I said, popping in the scary movie I'd let Parker pick.
"I can't believe I let you talk me into one of these stupid slasher movies."

"Don't worry, Ash. It's my job as your boyfriend to protect you,"
he said, winking.

"Yeah, is it your job as my boyfriend to be super cheesy now too?"
I asked with a laugh.

"Com' on! It wasn't that bad," he yelled, throwing a couch pillow
at me.

"Whatever you say, let's just watch the movie."

Burying my head into his chest, I watched out of the corner of my
eye as the bad guy entered through the front door of the house.

"Look behind you!" Parker yelled at the TV, neither of us aware
that Parker's older brother, Kyle, had entered the house.

"I don't think Mom and Dad would approve of you two sucking
face on their couch," Kyle said, flipping on the lights.

"Fuck, Kyle! You scared the shit outta us!" Parker yelled after I'd
jumped three feet away from him. "And, we weren't 'sucking face.'"

"Yeah, OK, whatever you say, Park," he said, stepping into the
kitchen. "Keep the lights on. Mom asked me to keep an eye on you two,
but I don't really feel like playing babysitter. Oh, and watch the language,
Little Brother," he taunted.

"We're fifteen, Kyle. I think we'll be fine." Parker was right, every-
thing was fine for the rest of the night—it wasn't until the early hours
of the morning when everything went horribly wrong.

Waking to the sound of my phone ringing, I frantically looked
around the room before realizing I'd left it in my purse. Taking
a moment to wipe the sleep from my eyes, I hopped off the bed,
grabbing my purse from the floor. Glancing at the phone, I was
surprised I'd missed four calls and seven text messages from Brad.
Opening the screen to read the messages, the phone flickered
with another incoming call.

"How the fuck are you awake? It's seven in the morning on a Saturday. You were drunk as a skunk less than six hours ago," I said, answering the call.

"Ash, what the fuck happened last night? I woke up feeling like I'd been roofied, but I'm in my own bed and still wearing my Peter Pan tights."

"Relax, you just drank your weight in caramel apple martinis. Carson and I dropped you off at your house shortly after midnight. I made sure you made it inside safely."

"Phew. That's a fucking relief," he sighed.

"Glad I could be of assistance, now if you're done, I'm going back to bed," I said.

"I'm sorry, I didn't realize the time. I hope I didn't interrupt sexy time with Doctor C," he chuckled.

"Goodbye, Bradley. Take two aspirin and drink a glass of water. You'll thank me later," I said, avoiding his comment.

"Bye. Thanks, Ash," he said, ending the call.

CARSON

*E*VEN THOUGH IT was the weekend and I was on-call at the hospital, I decided to go into the office to take care of some things that I'd left during the week. Sitting down at my desk, the folder with Ashlynn's case caught the corner of my eye as if it were taunting me. Scanning through the pages once again, I still couldn't find anything that stuck out.

Even though I knew I should just let it go, I decided to try the phone number that was scrawled on the back just once more. After three rings, I was just about to hang up when a male voice answered the call. "This is Parker Flynn, how can I help you?" he said.

Recognizing the name, I knew the number belonged to Ashlynn's ex-husband. "Hello, Mr. Flynn, I'm sorry to inconvenience you, but I'm a doctor calling from St. Therese's Hospital in regard to a Ms. Ashlynn Sommers."

"OK, I don't understand. Is Ashlynn all right? Are you her

doctor?"

"Oh, yes, Ashlynn is physically fine," I said, not wanting to worry him. "I'm just calling because I've recently taken her on as a patient and she suggested I give you a call," I lied, knowing I was not only risking my career, but also any future I had with Ashlynn. It was a risk I was willing to take.

"Ashlynn gave you my number?" he asked, sounding skeptical. "I have to be honest here, Doc. I don't know how I would be of any assistance to you or to her. We haven't been married in years."

"I just think you could provide me with some insight, that's all. I was hoping you might be able to come down to my office and meet with me?" I asked, hoping he'd agree.

"I don't know," he said, hesitating. "My wife is expecting a baby any day now, and I really just don't have a lot of extra time to spare. Besides, I'd really like to speak to Ashlynn before I agree to see you."

"No, no. That won't be necessary. Actually, on second thought, you're a busy man. We can try and set something up after your baby is born. Sorry to take up your time," I said.

"Wait, I'm sorry, I didn't catch your name," he said as I ended the call.

"That wasn't your finest moment, Carson," I said to myself, knowing I was playing a volatile game of Russian roulette with my career.

"You talking to yourself again, Brother," Camden said breaking me from my thoughts.

"Hey, just deep in this case file. What's going on?" I asked, surprised to see my brother at the hospital.

"Sorry, I saw your door was partially open. I wasn't even sure if you'd be in here today," he said, walking into the office.

"Yeah, I just had some cases that needed my attention."

"I still don't understand what you're doing here, though," I said again.

"I came in to speak with the director of the pediatrics department. Turns out you're not the only Doctor Foster that this fine hospital is interested in."

"Oh yeah?" I asked. "You get offered a position?"

"Sure did. I think I'm going to take it too. It'd be nice to stick around town for a while this time. Traveling the world playing a superhero doctor has its perks, but I miss my son. I think it's time to be a superhero dad for once," Cam said.

"Look at you finally growing up. And, Jade doesn't have anything to do with this decision?" I pried.

"Honestly, I haven't told her about it. But, I don't think she'll be opposed to having me around more," he admitted.

"Just as I suspected," I said, nodding.

"What do you say we get out of here, and grab a beer at Encore? We can catch the end of the football game, and you can tell me all about your date from the other night," Cam suggested.

"Um, I don't know. I have a lot of work I need to get done around here," I said, remembering running into Ashlynn the last time I'd been at Encore.

"Com' on! It'll still be there on Monday. We haven't gone out in years. I miss you, Brother," he nearly begged.

"Ok, fine. If you insist. Just give me a few minutes to finish up here. I'll be right behind you," I promised.

"All right, but don't take too long. You know I don't like drinking alone," he laughed, stepping out of my office.

Shutting the door behind my brother, I grabbed the file and stepped over to the shredder. I needed to rid myself of the folder and everything that reminded me of Ashlynn Sommers.

"THIS PLACE HASN'T changed since college," Camden said, as I grabbed the bar stool next to him. "Those were the good ol' days."

"Yeah, I'm pretty sure that's still the same bottle of absinthe sitting on the top shelf over there," I laughed, pointing out the half-full bottle.

"I remember we were sitting at these very stools when Jade and Marissa strutted in here like they owned the place," he reminisced.

"That they did," I chuckled.

"Sorry, I probably shouldn't have brought her up," he said, sympathy in his tone.

"Nah, it's OK. I'm in a good place now. It's been a long time," I reassured him.

"You do definitely seem to be in a better place. Could that be because of the mystery lady that you've been seeing? How'd your date go?"

"I thought things were going well, but it turns out she has more demons than I do. I can't get her to open up to me and it's killing me," I admitted.

"Have you opened up to her?" Camden said, throwing my words back at me.

"Well, no, but I'm not the one who's holding back. She's been keeping something buried inside her for years."

"Yeah, and how do you know this?"

"From the moment I met her, I just knew there was something holding her back. Call it an intuition, I guess. I'm drawn to her."

"Sounds like you're trying to doctor her."

"I'm not. This is different, Cam. I've never crossed a line with my patients. I've always been professional and not gotten overly involved with any of them. And, believe me, many of them have tried. I've had more than one patient think that since I'm a sex therapist that I'll cure them with my dick."

"Sounds like some of the mothers I have to deal with. I can only assume it's our dashing good looks," he laughed, chugging back the rest of the beer he'd been drinking.

"I take back what I said earlier, you really haven't changed, Bro," I joked, slapping him on the back.

"What can I say? Old habits die hard," he shrugged. "Seriously though, maybe you just need to give her some space."

"I think it's best if I just forget about her. I got a call from the facility in Minnesota anyway. They want me to come out next week to check it out."

"That's great. I know it's what you've wanted for a long time. But, Carson, is it what you still want?"

"Honestly, I'm not sure anymore. But, if Ashlynn can't open up then I need to do what's best for both of us and walk away."

"Why don't you tell her your secrets. Maybe then she'll tell you hers."

ASHLYNN

NEARLY TWO WEEKS had passed since the Halloween party. I'd tried calling and texting Carson a few times in the days following the party, but each time they went unanswered. I even tried cornering him at work the following week, but he'd told me he wasn't interested in talking. He even went so far as to suggest contacting his assistant if I needed to communicate with him regarding business matters.

"Word from the break room is Doctor Sexy will be leaving us soon," Brad said, waltzing into my office.

"Get in here and close the door behind you," I said, not wanting anyone to eavesdrop on our conversation. "Now, where'd you hear that?"

"His assistant, Danielle, told me that he's out of town checking out a new hospital near the Twin Cities," he gabbed.

"Since when does Carson's assistant give you all the gossip?" I asked.

"Since she decided she wanted to hook me up with her very available and very hot brother," he replied, fanning himself.

"I should've known," I chuckled.

"Did I mention he's super hot? She showed me his Instagram. He could be a cover model for one of those romance novels you're always reading, Ash."

"Correction, the romance novels we're always reading," I corrected, placing an emphasis on "we're."

"Fine. Since you seem to be missing the point here–the romance novels WE'RE always reading. You happy now?"

"Very," I said, pleased with myself. "You may continue now. Have you met him?"

"No, she's going to give him my number. Pray that he actually calls. I really think he could be the one!" he said, excitedly.

"How do you know that? You haven't even met him yet. What's his name? I want to look him up."

"Ned? No, Nate. No, that's not right either. Maybe it was Neil," he said, scratching his chin.

"You think you should actually get his name before you determine he's your soulmate?" I suggested.

"Meh. Just semantics," he said. "Oh, and Danielle also mentioned that the usually chipper Doctor Foster has been in a real foul mood since Halloween. Don't suppose you know anything about that, do you?" he asked, leaving the office before I had a chance to get any further information about Carson.

Before I had much more time to mull over what Brad had just told me, my cell vibrated on my desk. Seeing that it was Parker, I sent it to voicemail. He'd called a few times over the last few weeks, but I hadn't felt like talking to him. I knew that was selfish of me, but I wasn't in the mood to take any trips down memory lane.

Before I had a chance to check the voicemail, my office phone rang beside me.

"Yes," I said, picking up the phone.

"Ms. Sommers, Parker Flynn is on the line for you. Would you like me to send it through to your office?" my assistant asked.

"Yes, please. I'll take the call. Thank you," I said, before Parker was patched through the line.

"Parker? Sorry I haven't called you back. I've just been really busy lately. What's going on? What's been so urgent?" I asked.

"Listen, Ash, we can talk about that later. I'm calling about something else right now. I don't even know how to say this," he stumbled, sounding shaken.

"Parker, what's wrong? You're scaring me?"

"It's Kyle," he said, just hearing his brother's name sent a shiver down my spine. "He's dead."

"What? What do you mean? Kyle can't be dead," I said as the room started to spin around me.

"His girlfriend found him earlier today. The medical examiner is doing an autopsy, but it looks like he had an aneurysm burst sometime in the middle of the night."

Taking a deep breath, I wasn't sure how to react to the news. I hated that Parker was suffering, but there's no way I would ever grieve for Kyle.

"What can I do?" I asked, not knowing what else to say.

"Please say you'll come to the service. I know you and my brother weren't all that close, but I'd like it if you came. Plans aren't finalized yet, but the service will be early next week. I can call you back with the details."

"Park, I really wish I could come, but unfortunately, I have a conference all next week. It's been on my calendar for almost a year. I can't back out of it now. You know I'll be there in spirit though," I lied. Hanging up the phone, I rested my head against my palms, trying to make sense of everything Parker had just told me. Kyle Flynn was gone.

fifteen

ASHLYNN

*D*RESSED IN ALL black, I stood behind a large oak tree, watching as the last of the mourners retreated to their cars. The shadow of my breath danced before me in the crisp, late November air.

My parents were the last to leave, offering their condolences to Parker, my ex, and his sister, Vanessa. The two siblings were left alone in the rural cemetery to say their final goodbyes. Vanessa's sobs echoed through the barren trees as Parker kneeled on the freshly covered grave.

Just because I wouldn't allow myself to shed a tear for Kyle Flynn, it didn't mean that I didn't deeply hurt for Parker and Vanessa. They'd already buried both their parents, and now they were saying goodbye to their brother. Even though Kyle was ten years older than Parker and nearly thirteen years older than Vanessa, the three got along, more than just siblings, but also as best friends. There was a time when I'd fit into their little squad.

When Parker called to tell me the news of Kyle's passing, I was more than a little shocked. Truthfully, I tried not talking about Kyle–especially not with Parker. Just his name left me feeling guilty and afraid. I wasn't quite sure how to react, but I offered my sympathy for my ex-husband's sake. When he asked if I'd make it to the service, I quickly hunted for an excuse and told him I'd be out of town for a work conference.

I hadn't lied to him. I wasn't planning on going at all, but I guess I had to see it for myself—the casket, the grave, the final resting spot of Kyle Flynn.

Biting my bottom lip, I refused to shed a single tear. You aren't going to let him take you there again, I kept repeating to myself. *Not now. Not ever.*

After several minutes, Parker and Vanessa got up and walked hand-in-hand back to the car. I waited as Parker brushed the newly fallen snow from the windshield before getting into the car and driving off.

Finally, alone in the cemetery, I walked over to the gravesite, my heels crunching in the snow. Momentarily, I regretted coming alone. My parents would've been a shoulder to cry on, but they didn't know the whole truth. I'd told them the same lie as I'd told Parker. As far as they knew, I was hundreds of miles away in south Florida.

I'd made a decision all those many years ago to keep my secret. As a teenager, I thought my parents might've blamed me even though I knew now that wouldn't have been the case. But, I couldn't tell them now. My mother would never forgive me for keeping this secret from her for so long. And then there was also Parker. If he would've ever known the side of Kyle that I'd known, it would've broken him. I never told him my version of Kyle and I never could.

I had wanted to tell Carson. I wished he was standing at my

side, but instead I ran from him. I'd come very close to telling him everything while wrapped in his arms at the ball, as I desperately wanted to give him all of me. I wanted him to finally be the one to take me there, but in the end, I was too afraid–I was always too afraid. It was too late now. I couldn't even get him to return my calls. Soon, he'd be moving to Minnesota and I'd be nothing but a distant memory.

The secrets I'd kept for all those years were now buried with Kyle Flynn and that's where they would have to remain–forever.

Standing at the site for a moment longer, I startled at the sound of someone walking up from behind. Turning to see who was approaching, I was surprised to see it was Carson.

"What are you doing here?" I asked, my body shivering from the cold air.

"I thought maybe you could use a friend," he said, giving me a half-smile.

"How-how did you know I was here?"

"Call it an intuition," he shrugged, removing his black wool coat and placing it over my shoulders.

"Thank you," I whispered, blanketing myself in its warmth.

"I wasn't sure if I should come. I figured you would've said something if you wanted me here, but I didn't think you should be alone either. I hope I made the right decision," he added, his eyes pleading for confirmation.

"It's OK. I'm glad you're here. I just don't understand how you knew," I said, shaking my head in disbelief. "You haven't returned any of my calls and your assistant told Brad that you were out of town."

"I never made it to the airport. I was on my way, but I changed my mind. I came back to talk to you. When I got to your office, I overheard you on the phone with Parker. I heard you offer your condolences before you told him that you'd be out of town for a conference over the weekend. I couldn't remember your mentioning anything about a conference, so I checked with your assistant and she confirmed that your calendar was open. I wanted to ask you about it, but I wasn't sure if you'd even pick up your phone if I called," he explained with frustration in his voice. "The next morning, I saw the obituary in the newspaper. I made a note of the service time."

"I'm sorry for how things ended that night," I said, hoping he'd understand.

"Shhh. Don't even worry about it," he whispered.

"I still don't quite understand, though. You came back to talk to me? I thought you hated me. You haven't spoken to me in days."

"Oh, Ash, I definitely don't hate you. I was frustrated and probably didn't handle the situation as I should have. I was going to reach out last week but then something happened that demanded my full attention. I haven't meant to avoid you."

"It's OK. I deserved it. I haven't been honest with you. I haven't been honest with anyone for a long time," I admitted.

"If you want to talk, I can listen. I don't want to pressure you anymore though. If you want to stand here in silence, then we can do that too," he said, placing his hand on my shoulder. "If you'd rather be alone, I can leave. But, I hope you'll let me stay," he added, his eyes filled with hope that I wouldn't turn him away again.

"No, please stay. I just don't know what to say. There's just so much. I don't even know where to begin," I said, struggling to keep the tears at bay.

"Why don't you start from the beginning then?" he said, offering me a fresh hanky from his pocket.

"I don't think I can. I'm falling for you Carson, and I'm not supposed to fall. I can't fall. I'm broken and if you ever learned the truth you wouldn't want anything to do with me. You can't fix me. Not like you fix your patients," I said, tears now streaming down my cheeks.

"I've already told you, Ashlynn, you're not like my patients. You are so much more to me than that. I will never walk away from you," he said, sincerity in his tone. "We all have our secrets we'd rather keep buried, but I care about you, Ashlynn. I care about you a lot. I know you're afraid to take the next step in whatever we are, but I want so much more with you."

I couldn't do it anymore. I couldn't keep this secret buried inside me any longer. Taking a deep breath, I crumpled to the cold, frozen ground as a loud shriek wracked my body. Quickly kneeling on the ground beside me, Carson engulfed me in his arms. Burying my head in his chest, I did as he asked and started at the very beginning—telling him about that dark Halloween night so long ago.

"YOU CAN TAKE my bed if you want it. I'll sleep on the floor," Parker said after we'd finished watching the movie.

"You don't have to do that. I brought my sleeping bag with me," I said, pointing toward the corner of the room where my plaid sleeping bag sat with the rest of my things.

"Don't fight me on this, Ashlynn. No girlfriend of mine is going to sleep on the floor. We can share the bed if you want, though?" he suggested with a wink.

"Parker Andrew! You know I'm not that kind of girl!" I yelled, swatting him on the arm.

"I know, I know! I was only kidding! I would never pressure you into doing something that you didn't feel was right. You know that, right?"

"I know you wouldn't. I trust you," I said, giving him a peck on the cheek. "I'm going to go get ready for bed. I'll meet you back in your bedroom."

After spending several minutes in the bathroom, brushing my teeth and changing into my pajamas, I opened the door to a dimly lit hallway. Knowing my way around the Flynns' house, I didn't bother to turn on a light before tip-toeing out into the hall.

"Why are you being so quiet?" Kyle asked, standing in his bedroom doorway. Kyle moved back to his parents' house after graduating from business college nearly a year ago. He'd recently accepted a position as a manager at a local hotel, but Parker had said he wasn't making enough to get a place of his own yet.

"Shit, Kyle, you scared me! Don't you know it's not nice to creep up on girls in the dark–especially on Halloween!"

"Sorry, Ash," he said, walking toward me. "Have I told you before how pretty I think you are?"

"Kyle Flynn! Are you drunk?" I asked, his breath smelling of alcohol.

"Only for you, Beautiful," he said, falling into me.

"OK, Kyle. I think you need to go back into your bedroom, and sleep it off," I suggested.

"Yeah? Will you help me to bed? I think I'm drunk," he said.

"That's for sure," I sighed, leading him back to his bedroom.

"So, you like my brother, huh?" He stuttered.

"Of course, I like your brother. What kind of question is that?" I asked, defensively.

"I bet you really like me more. I'm a man, Ashlynn. Parker is just a boy with so much to learn. I can give you so much more."

"Kyle, you're embarrassing yourself," I said as he plopped down into his bed, pulling me with him.

"Say you want me, Ashlynn. Say it!" he demanded, pulling the strap of my tank top down, exposing my bare chest.

"Kyle, you're my boyfriend's brother. Why are you doing this?" I asked, realizing I hadn't actually told him no. "Parker is going to come in here looking for me any minute now," I said, praying he'd walk through the door. This was wrong. Why wasn't I demanding he let me go?

"Ha! Parker has been asleep since the minute his head hit the pillow. I made sure he was sleeping before I came looking for you," he admitted, pinning me beneath him.

"I saw you kissing him earlier. Was he your first kiss?" he asked.

"Yes," I responded, squirming under his weight.

"Looks like it's going to be a night of many firsts for you then, Pretty Girl. I bet you'll like it dirty," he said, slipping a hand down my pajama bottoms.

"MY BODY BETRAYED me that night. I hated what he was taking from me—what he was doing to me, but some sick part of me liked it. As much as I knew it was wrong, I liked it. I liked the way he made me feel inside. I fucking liked it, Carson!" I confessed, surprised when he didn't push me away for being a vile person. "I ended up going home that night because I knew I couldn't be in that house–not with him. Not with either of them. I went home and took a shower, hoping to wash the demons away. I cried on the shower floor for over an hour. I vowed then to never let my body betray me again. As a punishment and out of guilt for liking what he'd done to me, I would never again let myself feel pleasure from sex. To this day, I've kept that promise to myself. No matter how much I may want it."

Carson held me in silence for a moment longer as I gathered my composure. "It's a good thing that bastard is buried six feet below us because I'd probably kill him myself," Carson growled after I'd come clean and told him the gruesome details of that night.

"I understand if you don't want anything to do with me now," I cried.

"Why would you say that? Kyle Flynn took advantage of a fifteen-year-old girl. He should've spent the last years of his life behind bars. Why didn't you tell anyone sooner?"

"I was ashamed. I never told him 'no.' I let him do those things to me," I said, tears streaming down my cheeks.

"And, you've kept these secrets locked up inside since that night? Not even telling Parker?" Carson asked.

"God no. It would've killed him. He looked up to Kyle. He would've been devastated," I said, the memories of that awful night flooding back.

"Thank you for trusting me with your secrets. I don't intend on fixing you, but if you let me I think we can begin to heal–together. I'm all in, Ashlynn," he said, placing a soft kiss on my forehead. "What do you say we go sit in the car where it's warmer? If you want to talk more, that's fine. If not, I can take you home."

"I think that sounds perfect," I said, allowing him to help me get up. We walked together back to our cars, never looking back.

sixteen

CARSON

GETTING INTO THE car, I cranked up the heat to full blast before turning to face Ashlynn who was wiping the tears from her eyes.

"Do you want to talk about it anymore? Or would you like a ride home? I don't think you should be driving," I said out of concern.

"No, it's OK. We can talk more. I'm sure you have so many questions," she said, nervously biting her lip.

"Like I told you before, I don't want to pressure you. You can tell me whenever and whatever you'd like," I said, taking her hand in mine.

"No, it's OK. I want you to know. Ask me anything," she said, taking a deep breath.

"OK, as long as you're sure. If anything makes you uncomfortable you tell me–anything at all," I assured her.

"OK, I promise, I'll tell you," she agreed.

"OK, well you mentioned you were punishing yourself? Never allowing yourself to feel pleasure during sex? Was that just with Parker? Is that why you two divorced?"

"It started with Parker, yes. I never told him about that night, so I had to go on pretending as nothing had changed between the two of us. Truthfully, everything changed that night. Every time I looked at him, I would see his brother's eyes. Every time he spoke, I would hear his brother's voice," she said with pain in her voice.

Grabbing her hand more firmly to show my support, I asked her another question—not knowing if I was truly ready for the answer. "And, after Parker?" I asked.

She sighed uneasily before answering. "Well, I'm not a born-again virgin, if that's what you're asking. It'd probably be better if that were the case," she exhaled. "After Parker and I got divorced, I thought maybe I could finally try to heal. It'd been years since that Halloween night, and I thought, just maybe, I was ready to move past it. I really tried to enjoy sex. Honestly, I probably tried too hard. I'm not proud of the woman I became—having more meaningless sex than I ever care to admit. As a counselor, I should've definitely known it was wrong—known the dangers. And, I do, but I didn't care."

She paused for a moment to collect her thoughts. Not knowing what to say, and not wanting to come across as too judgmental, I gave her the time she needed to gather herself. Truthfully, I needed the silence to collect my own thoughts as well.

"Don't worry, I'm safe and I do get tested regularly," she continued, knowing the physician in me was concerned about her health.

"So, you're still punishing yourself for feeling something that night even though you want to move past it?"

"That pretty much sums it up. I've even tried every self-pleasure device in the complete sex toy catalog. You should see my full treasure chest in the bedroom. I bet it'd even make a sex therapist blush," she said, a hint of a smile forming on her lips.

As much as I was trying to keep this conversation platonic, the thought of Ashlynn pleasuring herself was causing a strain in my pants.

"Are you sure you're using them right?" I muttered rather thoughtlessly.

"Of course," she laughed, her cheeks slightly reddening. "I might not have become a fancy specialist such as yourself, but I did manage to pass one or two anatomy classes–with A's, might I add."

"I'm sorry, I didn't mean to just blurt out like that," I apologized. "I must've come across as insensitive to your plight. I just know a thing or two about how to please a woman–professionally speaking, of course."

"Well, if you're offering your 'professional' assistance," she said, flirtatiously.

"Ashlynn, don't say what you don't mean," I warned, reaching up to loosen my tie only to realize I wasn't wearing one.

"Getting hot over there, Doc?" she sassed.

"Maybe just a little," I said, turning down the heat.

"Carson, I can guarantee you one thing. Since that day, I'm in control of what I want, and I never say something I don't mean," she said, squeezing my hand. "Now, would you like to go back to my place where we can finish this conversation? We can order takeout or something. I'm just ready to leave this place–and Kyle Flynn–in the past."

"I think that sounds like a perfect idea," I said with a feeling of satisfaction in my voice.

♥

I'D ALL BUT insisted on leaving Ashlynn's car at the cemetery, and driving her back to her place, but she assured me that she'd be fine. After several minutes of arguing back and forth, I reluctantly agreed.

Stopping at Franny's for a pizza and before meeting Ashlynn back at her house, I sat in the car for a moment, trying to gather my thoughts. I had to make sure I was there for Ashlynn in a way she'd never experienced before. She'd dropped a lot for me to take in back at the cemetery, and although it was difficult to hear, I was relieved that she'd finally let me in. I couldn't let her run away–not again.

"Hey Franny, can I get a large pepperoni pizza with extra cheese?" I asked, waving at Joe who was busily preparing orders back in the kitchen.

"A large?" she questioned, raising her brow. "I hope you're sharing it with the pretty gal I met the other day. She seemed like a genuine, young lady, Carson."

"Yes, it's for Ashlynn. And, yes, she's pretty great."

"Carson Foster, I think you're smitten. I haven't seen you like this in years. I'm so happy to see that gleam in your eyes again. Your mother would be so proud of you if she were still with us."

"Thanks Franny, I sure hope so," I said, losing myself in memories of my mother.

"Something else on your mind, Carson?" Franny asked, always being able to read my brother and me.

"Marissa has finally been accepted by that facility in Minneapolis. They offered me a position at the nearby hospital. In fact, I was supposed to be there right now finalizing everything and signing my contract. It's what I've wanted for a long time."

"That's great, Sugar. But why do I have a feeling it's not what you still want?"

"I do, it's just I haven't told Ashlynn about her yet. I wasn't quite sure how to tell her. It's never seemed like the right time to dredge up our past," I explained. "I haven't told her about the new job yet either."

"Carson, you know you're like a son to Joe and me, right?" she asked.

"Yes, I know. And, I love you both for it," I said with a faint smile.

"Then you'll understand when I give it to you straight? You know the only things I go around sugar-coating are my famous Christmas cookies now," Franny said.

"Let me hear it, Franny," I replied.

"Miss Ashlynn deserves to know your past. It shaped the man you are today, you know," she advised. "She also deserves to know what your plans are for the future, Carson."

"I know you're right, but it's been a long road to get her to finally open up to me. I'd hate to lose her now because of something like this."

"If it's meant to be, then you won't lose her," she said, patting the top of my hand.

"Thanks, Franny. You always know what to say even if I may not want to hear it."

"Comes with age, Sugar," she said, grinning. "Now let me check to see if Joe has that pizza ready yet." Before she had time to step into the kitchen, Joe came through the swinging doors holding a large pizza box and a brown paper bag.

"Here you go, Son. I threw in an order of garlic bread and two pieces of strawberry rhubarb pie. Franny just baked it fresh today," Joe said, handing over the food.

"Thanks, guys. How much do I owe you for everything? And, don't say nothing."

"Nothing," they both said in unison.

"You two will never listen," I laughed, tossing two twenty-dollar bills on the counter.

seventeen

CARSON

*P*ULLING UP INTO Ashlynn's driveway, I was pleased to see she'd made it home safely. I wouldn't know what I'd do if anything happened to her. Even though she'd told me some pretty troubling things about her past, I knew I still needed her in my life–after all, we'd both been hiding some skeletons in our closets. Stepping out of the vehicle, I grabbed the pizza and beer from the back. Realizing what Franny said was only right, I knew I had to tell Ashlynn about my mother, my past with Marissa, and my impending job out-of-state.

"One of these days, you're going to let me take you on a proper date," I said, as she opened the door.

"You brought beer and pizza! What could possibly be more proper than that?" Ashlynn quipped, taking the piping hot boxes from my hands.

"Oh, I don't know–dinner and a movie? Dancing? Wine tasting? A hot-air balloon ride over Sedona?" I joked.

"Sedona? That seems pretty specific. If I didn't know any better I'd think you saw that date on 'The Bachelor,'" she giggled.

"What can I say? It's my guilty pleasure. Plus, I heard the chicks dig it," I laughed with a shrug.

"Well, you heard right. I dig it," she said, raising her hand.

"Already so much in common then," I teased. "Tell me you watch 'Monday Night Football' and we'll be the perfect pair.

"Mmmm, sorry, I think you're on your own there, Doc. Besides, any true Bachelor fan knows the two programs are on at the same time."

"Caught me, but there's always DVR," I said, shrugging.

Remembering where Ashlynn kept her paper plates, I took out a few from the cupboard as she opened two beer bottles. Sitting down at the table, we both grabbed two slices of pizza.

"What are you doing with those boxes in the corner?" I asked inquisitively.

"Oh, I dragged my Christmas decorations up from the basement. I thought maybe you could help put my tree up," she said with a smile before taking a small sip of beer.

"You want to put up your Christmas tree? You do realize it's not even Thanksgiving yet?"

"I'm aware," she said sheepishly. "Honestly, I usually put it up the day after Halloween. It's very therapeutic for me. I just didn't feel like it this year–with everything that's happened between us. Honestly, I guess I was hoping that eventually you'd be here helping me."

"How can I say no then?" I asked, overjoyed that she was letting me into her life.

"Well, I mean, you could, but then I'd have to throw this stocking at you," she laughed, rolling it into a tight ball.

"OK, OK, I concede. Where do I start?" I asked, covering my face in mock defense.

"Let's eat the pizza before it gets cold and then you can help me carry the rest of the boxes up from the basement."

"There are more?" I questioned.

"Oh yeah. Probably at least twenty!"

"Twenty boxes of Christmas decorations?" I asked in disbelief.

"Yeah. Why? Is that a lot?" she said, taking a bite of pizza.

"Yeah, I'd say. Unless your name is Elf and you live at the North Pole with Santa." I joked.

"Hardly," she laughed. "I've just always really liked Christmas. My mom really gets into it too. It's one of the few things we seem to agree on. Every year on the weekend before Christmas we spend two entire days baking. Well, I do more of the eating while she does the baking, but it's still one of my favorite times of the year," she reminisced.

"That sounds nice. You and your mom don't always get along?" I asked, hoping my question wouldn't offend her. Truthfully, it always shocked me when there were rifts between parents and their children. I would do anything to have my mother back with Camden and me. We may not have had many possessions growing up, but Mom definitely made up for it by showing us her love. I hoped that I would have that same type of relationship with my own children someday.

"We do. She just tends to nag me about everything and both my parents took it really hard when Parker and I divorced. I can't wait to see what they say when I take you to meet them," she said, grinning.

"Yeah? You're taking me to meet your parents now? I'd say that's a pretty big step, Miss Sommers."

Suddenly seeming unsure of herself, she tried backtracking. "I didn't mean tomorrow. Just, never mind. You don't have to meet them if you don't want to. I don't know what I was thinking," she mumbled.

"Ashlynn," I said, reaching for her hand across the table. "Of course, I'd love to meet your parents. In fact, you could call them over right now," I offered, hoping it would calm her nerves.

"Thanks, but that's OK. My place is far too much of a mess right now to have my mother over," she joked, as a piece of greasy pepperoni fell off the pizza she'd been holding.

"Crap! That's going to leave a stain," she huffed. "I just bought this shirt too. This is why I can't have nice things."

"I'm sure it won't be that bad," I said, reassuringly.

"Oh yeah. You know the secret to getting grease stains out of laundry?"

"Nope, you got me. I actually have no idea. I still throw my whites and colors all in together," I admitted with a chuckle.

"Right," she laughed. "If you'll excuse me, I need to get changed into something else that doesn't make me look like a messy toddler. Can I get you another beer while I'm up?"

"Sure, but I can grab it. Can I get you one?"

"Yeah, sure. You wouldn't have happened to pick up any dessert to go with this delicious meal, did you?" she asked, walking back to the bedroom.

"Do you think I would dare step into your house without a sugary dessert?" I yelled down the hall.

"You're a quick study, Dr. Foster. I think I'm going to like having you around," she said, peeking her head around the door.

"Yeah? I think I'm going to like being around, too," I responded, taking two more bottles of beer from the fridge. "I shouldn't actually be getting all the credit for the dessert though. You should really be thanking Franny and Joe. I guess they thought we both needed a fresh piece of rhubarb pie," I said, picking up the rest of the trash from the table.

"Strawberry rhubarb?" she yelled from the bedroom. "That's

my absolute favorite! Not too sweet and not too sour–the perfect blend," she added.

"I think you've said that about every kind of dessert," I laughed.

"I can't help it!"

Walking back into the kitchen, she'd changed into a pair of Rudolph pajama bottoms and a matching T-shirt. I couldn't help but laugh at her wardrobe selection.

"What?" she giggled. "If we're going to decorate this place like it should be done, then I needed to commit one hundred percent. I have a Grinch T-shirt in the bedroom that would probably fit you, if you'd like it."

"Nah, I'm good. I think I'm feeling festive enough without needing a costume," I said, drawing her in tightly against my chest. Feeling her heartbeat quicken with my touch, I knew she wanted to kiss me again as much as I wanted a second taste of her. I'd been imagining the taste of her lips on mine ever since her vanilla lip balm lingered on my lips for hours after we'd first kissed.

Ashlynn stood on her tiptoes as I clutched the nape of her neck, pulling her in for a kiss, this one more aggressive than the last. As our lips crashed together, my hands became entangled in her hair, only deepening our kiss. As much as I knew she wasn't ready to rush into anything, I craved her–every last piece of her. Finally, after what seemed like an eternity, I moved away from Ashlynn, knowing I had to get control of the situation. The electricity between us seemed inescapable.

"Are you trying to distract me, so I forget about the Christmas decorating?" she asked, trying to catch her breath.

Maybe? Did it work?" I questioned.

"Almost," she quipped. "Now let's get to work."

♡

ASHLYNN

"I THINK THAT'S all of them," I yelled down the stairs as Carson carried up the last of the boxes.

"That was a lot more than twenty," he huffed, setting the box in the living room. "I won't have to go to the gym for a week now."

"Shut up! It wasn't that bad!" I said, swatting him on the arm.

"How does one person even have this much Christmas stuff? I really think you could decorate the North and South poles and still not run out of ornaments!"

"I've been collecting it since I was a kid. Every year for Christmas, I would ask for more ornaments and decorations to add to my hope chest. Once I moved out on my own, it really snowballed–no pun intended," I giggled.

"Where do you even start?" he asked, scratching his chin.

"That's a silly question, Harvard grad! You always start with the Christmas tree!"

"Wait! The apparent queen of Christmas doesn't get a real tree?" he quizzed.

"No, I just put up the same artificial one each year. I never wanted to go alone to pick out a real one," I explained with sadness in my voice

"I think we should go get one then," he suggested.

"Nah, the fake one is fine. We don't have to go out. The tree farm is probably closed by now anyway," I rebutted.

"I think it's open for another forty-five minutes or so," he said, glancing at his watch. "Come on, I'll even splurge and buy you a hot chocolate."

"With extra marshmallows?" I asked, my voracious appetite suddenly aroused. This boy really did know how to play dirty. He knew chocolate–or any sugary confection for that matter–was my weakness. I'd just told him so.

"Well that's a given," he agreed. "Now what do you say?"

"Fine, you win, but I need to go change my clothes again!" I laughed. Clearly, I couldn't be caught in public wearing Rudolf across my heinie.

"Why? I think you're adorable just the way you are. Besides, it's the right time to be festive!" he encouraged.

"If you say so," I chuckled. "I'll just grab a hoodie then. I don't want to freeze out there!"

eighteen

ASHLYNN

I OPENED THE front door for Carson as he dragged the fresh pine into the house. Steve Urkel immediately jumped off his cat tower to come over and investigate.

"Get back, Urkel. I don't think you'll want to get a pine tree needle stuck in your nose," I laughed as the cat sniffed the tree.

"Are there any more bags in the car?" I asked Carson as he closed the front door behind him.

"No, I think we got all fifteen of them," he laughed. "I'm still not sure how a trip to the tree farm turned into a two-hour trip to the department store."

"Because I've never had a fresh tree before. I needed a new stand, new skirt, bigger lights, and a different topper," I explained.

"OK, fine. But, how do you explain the ten new ornaments?"

"It's obviously a bigger tree, Carson," I yelled as he stood the tree up in its stand.

"Oh OK. Something tells me you would've had enough in your

forty boxes already stacked around your living room."

"You hush!" I laughed. "Besides, this was all your idea. I was perfectly content on putting up my old, artificial tree. In fact, I think I'll still put that one up, too–maybe in the dining room by the sliding door."

"Let's just concentrate on this one first," he suggested, pointing to Steve Urkel who was busily climbing up the trunk of the tree. Good thing I bought that squirt bottle while we were at the store.

"Steve Urkel, you get down from there," I shouted as the cat momentarily paused to stare at me before climbing higher up the tree.

"I can tell this isn't going to go over so well," I said, sighing in defeat.

"He'll be fine as long as he doesn't chew on the cords like that poor cat in 'National Lampoon's Christmas Vacation,'" he snickered.

"I love that movie–or the part where the giant icicle goes through the neighbor's window," I giggled. "We can watch it if you want? I mean if you want to stay. I know it's getting late, and we have to work in the morning," I sidetracked.

"I'd love to," he answered with hesitation. "Why don't you start the movie and I'll go wash this sap off my hands," he chuckled, sticking his fingers together.

"I don't think we actually need to watch the movie. It appears we're already living it," I joked.

With the movie playing in the background, I threw a ball of wadded lights at Carson to get untangled. "What am I supposed to do with these?" he asked in mock horror.

"You graduated from medical school which means you had a surgical rotation. Now get busy and untangle those lights," I demanded.

"I probably should've paid more attention in that rotation," he muttered under his breath.

"What was that, Doc?" I asked with a laugh.

"Nothing. Absolutely nothing," he huffed. "Can I ask why we bought all new lights if I have to untangle the old ones anyway?

"Because I need both the big lights and little lights on the tree. Go big or go home, right?"

"Right now, I'm thinking home seems like the best option," he snickered.

"You don't mean that," I refuted.

"You're right, I don't. But this is still pretty awful," he admitted.

AFTER WE'D STRUNG the lights and garland on the tree, I picked up the first ornament from the box. "Before you hang that one, I have an early Christmas present for you," he said, picking up a medium-sized, wrapped box next to the arm of the chair. "Where have you been hiding that all this time," I asked, shocked that I hadn't noticed it before.

"What can I say? I'm just that good," he laughed, handing me the package.

"But, Christmas is still weeks away and I don't have anything yet for you. Are you sure you don't want to wait?" I asked.

"Don't argue with me, Ashlynn. Just open it," he instructed, kissing me on the tip of the nose.

"Fine," I said, ripping off the paper and opening the gift box. "Oh my god, I love it," I said, pulling out a beautiful, heart-shaped glass ornament. Taking a better look at it, I saw the inscription: Carson & Ashlynn—First Christmas Together.

"I don't know what to say," I said, a stray tear falling down my cheek.

"Say you'll be my girlfriend–say you'll be mine," he whispered, wiping a tear away with his thumb.

"I will," I whispered. "This is the sweetest, most caring thing that anyone has ever done for me. I don't deserve you, Carson Foster."

"I want to make traditions with you, Ashlynn Sommers. Good memories that will far outweigh the bad," he said, opening my heart wider to him. "I want to pick out the perfect Christmas tree with you every year on the first of November. I want to give you a different ornament each year that you'll hang on the tree first. And, last but certainly not least, I want to make love to you under the twinkling lights until dawn brings us a new day."

"I think I want that too," I said, his lips meeting mine, our tongues entwining together.

Placing lingering kisses on my lips, Carson slowly pulled away. "You think, or you want, Ashlynn? Those words have two entirely different meanings. I need you to be sure."

"I want you, Carson."

Hearing my words, Carson wrapped his arms around my waist, and slowly pulled my shirt up by its hem, unveiling my red and black satin bra.

"Well aren't you just the most delectably wrapped package," he growled. "You lied when you said you didn't have a present for me."

"I have a secret," I whispered, kissing him just below the ear. "The bottom matches the top."

"Fuck me. This I have to see," he groaned. Standing, I began teasing him by slowly untying my pajama bottoms letting them fall to my feet. Carson's jaw dropped as I stood there in only my bra and panties. Leaning back on his palms, I watched as his gray eyes took me in completely. Observing him as he watched me might have been the sexiest sight I'd ever witnessed.

"Come here," he said, tugging me into his lap. Stradling his legs, he peppered kisses across my chest and neck before capturing my lips with his. Pulling back, he looked me right in the eyes, his intensity catching me by surprise. "Are you sure this is what you want? I can wait for you as long as you need me to."

"Carson, I've never wanted anything or anyone so badly in my entire life. I want you. Please take me there," I nearly begged, my chest pressing against his. Trying to calm my nerves, my mind began to unravel as Carson reached behind me, unclasping my bra.

"Perfection," he moaned, rubbing his smooth palms across my chest. "Can I taste them?" he asked, seeking my approval once more.

"You don't have to ask each time you want to touch me. I'm fine. I promise I'll tell you if I need to stop," I reassured him.

Nodding in understanding, he gently sucked on both breasts before lightly biting down on my nipple. Not wanting to let the other go unnoticed, he used the pad of his thumb to gently flick the other sensitive bud.

Carson's hands and mouth hadn't moved south of my breasts, but I was convinced at that moment I could finally come with just that pleasure alone. Carson Foster was certainly good with his hands–just as I'd dreamed all those weeks earlier.

"Where are your vibrators," he asked, surprising me.

"In my bedroom, top dresser drawer," I panted. Before having a chance to ask any more questions, Carson was up and walking toward the bedroom. After just a few seconds, he returned with one of my vibrators.

"What are you going to do with that?" I asked, my breathing unsteady.

"I'm going to show you just how to work this thing," he said with a grin. "Now sit back and spread those beautiful legs for me."

Doing just as Carson instructed, I sat back on the couch, spreading my legs wide open for him, the only barrier between us was just the thin piece of satin of my underwear.

"As pretty as these are, I think they need to go," he said, rubbing his fingers across my covered pussy. Turning on the vibrator, he replaced his fingers with the toy, running it over my core.

"Please, Carson," I begged, already feeling sensations that were quite new to me.

"Lift up," he said, patting me on the side of the thigh. Lifting my hips as Carson instructed, he quickly peeled my underwear off my body, tossing them across the room with the rest of my clothing.

"Fuck, you're so ready. You're glistening," he growled, running the vibrator from the slit of my ass up to my pussy where the vibration alone nearly rocked me over the edge.

Spreading my legs further apart, Carson took that as a sign and glided the vibrator into my pussy stopping right over my clit.

Working the vibrator with one hand, Carson used his free hand to pinch and caress my pert nipples.

"Oh god," I moaned, causing him to pinch a bit harder.

"You like that?" he asked, sliding the vibrator even further into my pussy.

"Oh my god, Carson. I think I'm going to come," I said, right as he turned off the vibrator.

"Why-Why did you do that?" I protested, trying to catch my breath. "I was just about to have an orgasm. Why did you stop me?

"I just wanted to show you that you could do it," he said. "But there's no way I'm actually going to let you come unless it's around my cock."

Without hesitation, he yanked off his shirt, throwing it aside with the others. It was now my turn to take in the man that stood before me. His chiseled six-pack was everything I'd imagined it to be. His perfectly sculpted abs led right down to a mouth-watering V on his hips. I imagined using my tongue to trace the light trail of hair from the bottom of his abdomen that led to just below his belt.

"If you're done enjoying the previews, we can get ready for the show," he said, unbuckling his belt, letting his pants fall to the floor.

My eyes roaming over the bulge in his shorts, I motioned for Carson to come closer. Placing my hand on the band of his boxer briefs, I slowly pulled them down, exposing his fully erect cock. Noticing the glint on the head, I instinctively bent down and licked the tip. Looking up at him, I began bobbing my head up and down. "Oh fuck, Ashlynn. As perfect and unexpected as this is, I don't think I can hold out much longer," he moaned. "I need to be inside you."

Picking me up and carrying me back to the bedroom, he gently placed me on the center of the bed before crawling on top of me.

Looking at me with concern in his eyes, I answered him without having to hear his words. "Top drawer of the nightstand," I said.

Reaching over me, he opened the drawer, pulling out a foil-wrapped condom. Unwrapping it, he carefully sheathed his cock in its entirety before gently guiding himself into me. Exhaling sharply as he fully entered me, I moved slightly beneath him to fully open myself to his girth.

"Are you, all right?" he asked, sinking deeper into my pussy.

"So good," I moaned. "In fact, I've never felt better," I assured him.

Arching my back, Carson began sucking on my nipples. Rocking back and forth, the sound of his balls smacking against my ass had me on the precipice of my release. Digging my fingers into his back, he feverishly kissed me as he continued to fill me to the hilt with each thrust.

His breathing became ragged and I knew he was close to his

release. I'd been in this same position more times than I cared to admit, and each time I faked it just so the men could get it over with and leave. Not this time–not with Carson. This time it felt different. This time I wanted everything he could give me.

"Come for me, Gorgeous," he panted, pounding himself harder into my core. "I want to feel your pussy spasm around my cock. I want to feel you come for me."

"Please, don't stop! Oh god, I'm so close," I screamed, curling my toes in anticipation.

"We're going to do this together. You understand?" he asked.

Nodding my head, he reached down between us and began stroking my clit as he simultaneously slammed into my pussy once more, sending me over the edge. Rocking his hips back and forth once more, he came undone with his own orgasm. Resting my head against the pillow, I was overcome by emotion, tears streaming down my face.

"Are you OK? Did I hurt you?" Carson asked, rolling over onto his side.

"I'm fine," I said, wiping the tears from my eyes. "That was just so incredible. I didn't think I could ever feel that way. You made me feel that way. Thank you."

"No, thank you," he said with a grin, placing a kiss on my forehead. "You're the one who's incredible."

"Carson?" I said.

"Hmmmm?" he responded, sleepily.

"Will you stay here with me tonight?" I requested, knowing I'd never asked another man to stay in my bed overnight.

"Of course," he responded, pulling me as close as possible into him.

nineteen

ASHLYNN

*W*AKING UP JUST before my alarm, I was surprised to find myself alone in bed. Realizing that Carson may have had early morning rounds at the hospital, I decided to head to the kitchen in search of coffee and a note like the one he'd left the first night he'd brought me dinner.

Throwing on a pair of panties along with Carson's button-down shirt that he'd left on the floor, I went down the hallway, the aroma of freshly fried bacon wafting through the kitchen. I was pleasantly surprised to see Carson already making breakfast wearing only his pants. I stood for a moment taking in the sight before me and drooling as I gazed at his back and shoulder muscles as he precisely flipped pancakes into the air.

"That's pretty impressive, Dr. Foster. If the whole medical thing doesn't work out for you, it looks like you could have a career as a chef at Franny's," I laughed, as he flipped one last pancake.

"I didn't see you sneak up on me. I hope you enjoyed the show," he said, stalking toward me.

"Mmmhmmm, very much so," I moaned as he pulled me in for a gentle kiss. "Please tell me you brewed some coffee to go with all this food."

"I did. Let me pour you a cup," he said, handing me a warm mug.

"I think I may have actually stumbled upon the perfect man," I said, taking a sip of coffee. "I still don't know how you were able to stay single all these years."

"Just waiting for you–the perfect woman," he offered, winking.

"OK, I take it back. Now I know why you were single," I chuckled, playfully.

"You sleep OK?" he asked.

"Mmmhmmm, very well. Maybe the best I've slept in years, actually," I replied. It was true. I didn't think I'd ever slept as well as I had wrapped in the safety of Carson's arms. After our conversation the day before and what was to follow, I finally felt as though the world had been lifted from my shoulders. No more pretending. No more faking. No more lies.

"That's good. I thought maybe I'd been too rough with you," he said, flirtatiously.

"No, it was perfect. You were perfect," I promised, smiling up at him. "I hope you don't mind, but I borrowed your shirt. I thought you'd left it behind, and I didn't feel like digging for something else to wear."

"It's perfectly fine. And, if I must say so myself, you look hot as fuck in my shirt and those super sexy panties of yours," he growled. "I think we might have to both play hooky today, so I can take you back to the bedroom."

"I wish I could, but I have a massive workload on my schedule," I sighed, already dreading the day ahead.

"Well in that case, you better eat up," he said, interrupting me from my thoughts.

"Actually, I thought I'd just grab a doughnut on my way to work," I said, hoping I wouldn't offend Carson by turning down his cooking.

"A doughnut? Seriously, Ash, sit down. Let me pour you a glass of OJ. It's freshly squeezed."

Looks like I had one more embarrassing secret to share with Carson after all. "Fine, but you need to add some chocolate chips to those pancakes. I think there are some in the cupboard to your right," I explained, remembering I'd ordered some in my last grocery delivery.

Raising his brow, "OK, but why?"

Burying my face in my palms, "Because I'll only eat breakfast if it's in the form of a dessert," I giggled.

"I'm confused. I've seen you eat breakfast plenty of times."

"Yeah? And what did I eat?"

"Doughnuts, waffles a la mode, a scone," he responded.

"Mmmmhmmm. All desserts."

"Wait. I saw you eating toast in the cafeteria the other morning!" he yelled as if catching me red-handed.

"That's true, but what you failed to see was that it was smothered in cinnamon sugar," I added.

"You're adorable," he laughed, kissing my forehead. "Why just desserts?"

"Why not just desserts?" I asked, shrugging my shoulders. "It's something I've been doing since I was a kid. What other meal can you get away with eating just desserts? Seems pretty ingenious to me."

"Freakin' Einstein," he laughed. "Now let's find those chocolate chips!"

As Carson foraged through the cabinets in search of the

chocolatey morsels, I picked a piece of crispy bacon off the grid-
dle.

"I thought it was just desserts," he laughed.

"You have so much yet to learn, young grasshopper," I joked.
"Bacon is so much more than dessert. Bacon is life. Heaven even."

"Of course, it is, but I bet chocolate-covered bacon is even
better," Carson suggested, tossing the bag of chocolate chips in
my direction.

"You really are a quick learner," I giggled.

"What about whipped cream? Is that allowed at the breakfast
table?" he asked with a wink.

"Depends on what you have in mind."

"Why don't you come closer and find out," he teased.

Giving the can a quick shake, he tipped it over, outlining the
crease of my neck in the sugary confection.

"I'm going to get so sticky," I snickered.

"That's the plan," he chuckled, adding a dollop to the tip of
my nose.

"Something tells me the whipped-cream bikini was sexier
about twenty years ago."

"Mmmm, I think this is pretty damn sexy," he said, licking
the whipped cream off my neck. "But I do like where your mind
is at with the bikini," he added, unbuttoning my shirt, exposing
my bare chest.

Shaking the can once again, he tipped it over to squirt a dollop
onto each nipple before picking me up and setting me on the
kitchen island. "Lie back and lift your hips," he instructed, as he
pulled off my panties. Upending the can once more, he outlined
the lips of my pussy. Trembling with anticipation, I lifted my
head to watch him momentarily pause to enjoy his handiwork.

"You were wrong, Gorgeous. The whipped-cream bikini is

still fuckin' sexy," he growled, dropping his head to my pussy where he began skillfully tracing my outer lips with his tongue.

"Well that brings a whole new meaning to dessert at breakfast," I moaned, smiling lazily.

Delving his tongue into my center, he slowly sucked on my pulsating clit. After just a few moments, my body tensed, and heat radiated across my chest. I couldn't hold back any longer. Gone were the days of holding back, as my hips bucked, and I screamed out in pleasure. Carson continued his assault on my pussy until I began coming down from my orgasmic high.

Sitting up, I smiled as Carson's eyes were still fixated on the melting whipped cream on my chest. "Can I have a taste," I asked, pulling his lips toward mine. The taste of the whipped cream mixed with my wetness was intoxicating. I knew I needed more of Carson, and I needed him now. Work responsibilities be damned. Kissing his lips, I worked to unfasten his belt.

"I think it's time to take this back to the bedroom," I breathed through impassioned kisses.

"Not that I'm arguing, but I thought you said something about a massive workload," he mumbled.

"We can go into work late. I have a feeling the boss will approve it," I said, wrapping my legs around his torso. "Now please take me back to the bedroom!"

"You don't need to ask me twice," he groaned, assaulting my swollen lips once more.

MAKING IT INTO the office shortly after noon, I met with a few clients before heading to the staff lounge to refill my coffee.

"Sorry to burst your bubble, but the lounge is closed. There was a note on the door this morning about a burst pipe, or something. I guess we all have to use the lounge on the sixth floor," Brad said, stopping me in the hallway. "Had you actually been around this morning, you might have already known that though."

"I had an appointment this morning. I only worked a half day," I explained, hoping he wouldn't ask any more questions. "Sure, whatever you say, Ash. You haven't seen Carson around, have you? Evidently, he was out of the office this morning too."

"Oh, I'm not sure. Maybe he's still out of town," I suggested, hoping he bought it.

"Nah, his assistant said she's spoken to him, and he's definitely back in town." Sighing, I decided to come clean with Brad, after all, he was my best friend.

"Fine. I didn't want to say anything because I know you have a big mouth and I didn't really want the entire floor–let alone the entire hospital–knowing my business, but Carson and I spent the night and this morning together," I whispered.

"I knew it! You definitely have the glow of a woman who's been freshly fucked," he nearly shrieked.

"Shhhhhhhh! I don't want everyone knowing my business especially since Carson is technically my boss. We wouldn't want people getting the wrong impression," I scolded.

"OK, fine, but I still need the details. Please tell me Doctor Sexy is good in the sack," he said.

"Stop being ridiculous. I'm not discussing my boyfriend with you!"

"Ashlynn Jayne Sommers, did you just call Carson your boyfriend?" Brad squealed.

"I did," I said, grinning.

"Oh my god! It's about damn time you got your head out of your ass! I'm so happy for you!" he gushed. "Oh, and, thank you."

"Thank you? For what?" I asked, confusedly.

"Looks like I won the office pool," he bragged, checking the calendar on his phone. "Yep, sure did."

"Office pool? What are you talking about? You're not making any sense."

"Oh, you don't need to worry about everyone knowing about you and Carson. Everyone pretty much already knew something was going on. We had a pool going on guessing when you two would finally hook up. I had the last date picked so I automatically won. Thanks for being so stubborn, Bestie," he said, waltzing toward the nurses' station.

"Lunch tomorrow is on you," I yelled after him.

Turning the corner toward the sixth-floor lounge, I was surprised when I saw Carson standing there pouring a cup of coffee.

"That late night we had, catching up to you too?" I asked, rubbing against his ass as I walked behind him.

"My brother must be one lucky man if he had a late night with you," Camden said, turning to face me.

"Excuse me?" I said, my cheeks flushing from embarrassment.

"I'm sorry that was unprofessional of me. I'm Doctor Camden Foster, but I presume you already knew that," he said, extending his hand to me.

"That's funny, I think that's exactly the same way your brother introduced himself," I laughed, their similarities so uncanny.

Camden was as good-looking as his brother, but as he faced me, I noticed subtle differences: Carson's lips twitched when he smiled and the blue flecks in his eyes danced when he was excited about something.

"You must be Ashlynn?" he questioned.

"Yes, how did you know?"

"Carson has told me so much about you. I'm sorry for giving you the wrong impression at the skating rink all those weeks ago.

I heard I almost got my brother in big trouble. We haven't been down that road now for several years," he chuckled.

"It's OK. I'm glad to finally meet you. Now I know that Carson wasn't just telling me a story. He really does have a twin brother. But, I don't understand, why are you here at St. Therese? Oh god, I've been rambling this entire time. Is Carson OK?"

"Yes, don't worry, Carson's fine. I actually accepted a position in the pediatric department. Today is my first day. Just like my brother, not to mention it."

"Well we hadn't spoken for a few weeks until last night, and then we had a lot of ground to cover," I explained.

"Things are good now though between the two of you?"

"Yeah, they couldn't be better," I said with a smile.

"That's great. I'm happy to hear it. I was planning on heading down to see him in a bit. I'll have to tell him that his new lady tried flirting with me. That's sure to torture him," he chuckled.

"Oh god, I'm so embarrassed. I'm really sorry about that," I said, burying my face in my hands.

"Relax, Ashlynn, no problem. I'm just wanting to have a little fun with my brother, that's all."

"If you insist," I said, pouring out the rest of the coffee. "Anyway, it was nice to meet you, Camden. I'm sure I'll be seeing you around," I added, stepping back into the hallway.

CARSON

S TARING AT THE contract that was sitting on my desk when I arrived in the afternoon, I laughed at the irony of the situation. Since the accident, I'd been trying to get Marissa into a state-of-the-art, long-term care facility that specialized in traumatic brain injuries. Not only had one finally accepted her as a patient, but the nearby hospital was offering me a position in its psychiatric ward which meant I could move with her and oversee her care as I'd been doing for the last decade.

For over ten years, I'd been putting her needs before my own. Her parents had helped when they could, but they didn't have the means to care for her as I could. I'd made a promise to Marissa all those years ago, and until recently I thought I'd always keep that promise.

After the accident, I didn't put myself out there. I didn't want to date. I'd focused all my time and energy on Marissa's health and my career. I thought she was the love of my life and I wasn't interested in finding another–not until Ashlynn came into my life so unexpectedly.

Crumpling the sheet of paper that spelled out the terms of the position, I threw it across the room, landing at my brother's feet.

"What'd that piece of paper do to you?" he joked.

"You forget how to knock?" I asked, glaring at my brother.

"Nope. Just never have. Didn't see any reason to start now," he said, shrugging.

"What brings you by? I'm assuming by the scrubs that you decided to take the position in peeds?"

"Yeah, I started today. I think I'll like it here. It'll be nice working with you," he said, sitting on the edge of my desk. "Really though, what has you so bent-out-of-shape? After meeting a certain brunette upstairs, I thought I'd find you in a much better mood."

"Oh, you met Ashlynn, then?" I barked.

"Yeah, that's what I just said. She seems to think the two of you are back on track. Is that not the case?"

"No, we're good. She finally confided in me. We spent last night together actually," I confessed, exhaling sharply.

"That's great. I'm happy for you. You truly deserve it, Bro."

"Thanks, but that's the fucked-up part in all of this. You know the facility in Minneapolis finally accepted Marissa? I got a job there too. It's what I've wanted for fifteen fucking years–until now. I love Ashlynn, Cam." I said, admitting for the first time that I was in love with her.

"Whoa. Have you told her?" he questioned.

"No, I didn't even quite realize it until I just told you."

"Maybe it's time to finally let Marissa go. She'll be in good hands there," he said.

"But, I made her a promise. What kind of man would I be if I broke that promise?" I asked.

"Well, I think you should probably tell Ashlynn then! Lay it all out on the table, once and for all. Maybe she'll go to Minnesota with you."

"I can't ask her to uproot her entire life for me. That's not being fair of me to ask–especially under the circumstances."

"Life isn't fair, Brother. You of all people should realize that," he said with a sad smile.

"Yeah, it fucking blows, but you're right. I can't keep hiding this all from her."

"Just talk to her. I bet you're worrying for nothing."

"Yeah, I will soon," I said, rubbing my hands over my face.

When do they want you to start?"

"I'm supposed to be out there the first week in December, but I haven't signed the contract yet. They even wanted me to come out this weekend, but other obligations got in the way. They faxed the contract over earlier today."

Reaching into his pocket, Camden pulled out a pager. "Oh, I'm needed upstairs. Let me know if I can do anything to help. Love ya, Man," he said, turning to leave.

"Love ya, too. And, thanks, Cam," I said.

"Anytime," he said, shutting the door behind him.

Picking up my cell, I typed out a text to Ashlynn.

CARSON: *Hey Gorgeous, are you free tonight? I thought maybe I could take you out on a proper date?*

ASHLYNN: *Yeah, I should be done with my last appointment around 5:30 p.m. Do you want me to meet you in your office when I'm done?*

CARSON: *Sounds perfect. See you there.*

ASHLYNN: *Looking forward to it.*

CARSON: *Oh, and, Ash. I haven't been able to stop thinking about you and last night all day. ;)*

ASHLYNN: *Me neither. It was pretty great.*

♡

"ARE YOU FINALLY taking me on a genuine date?" Ashlynn asked, as we pulled out of the hospital's parking ramp and into heavy, five o'clock traffic.

"I was thinking we could try the new Italian restaurant downtown, if you're up for it."

"Sounds good to me. I'm starving. Someone kept me too busy for breakfast and lunch today," she said, grinning mischievously.

"Are you complaining?" I asked, turning to face her.

"Definitely not. I'd skip eating every day if we could have a repeat performance of this morning," she laughed.

"I'm sure that could be arranged, but first I think we need some nourishment. We need our energy for what I have in mind later," I teased.

"Mmmmm, I think I like the sound of that," she moaned in a lustful undertone.

"Ashlynn, don't be making sounds like that, or we might not make it to the restaurant."

"You're right let's talk about something else," she suggested. "How was the rest of your afternoon?"

"Ummm, it was OK," I lied, not ready to discuss Marissa or my impending job offer. "I heard you ran into Camden."

"Oh god, I swear I thought he was you," she said, covering her face in mock shame.

"What are you talking about?"

"Wait, he didn't tell you?" she asked.

"No, should he have told me?"

"No, forget I said anything. What did he say?"

"Seriously, what did you do?" I laughed.

"I may have rubbed up against him a little," she admitted, biting her lip. "I had to go upstairs for coffee because as you probably know the one on our floor was closed for maintenance. I saw him in the lounge and I just assumed it was you. You never told me that your brother was coming to work at St. Therese. To say I was a little surprised would be an understatement. I hope he didn't feel too violated."

"Ha! I think my brother will be fine, but he may need to wear a sign on his back, so he doesn't get any extra lovin' from my girlfriend."

"You're just as crazy as he is. Actually, I'm surprised he didn't say anything. He seemed pretty eager to torture you over it when I left the lounge."

"He probably got distracted. We started talking about something else when he came into the office," I explained.

"Anyway, It won't happen again," she insisted. "I can notice a few differences now."

"That's good, but there's a pretty obvious difference between the two of us," I added.

"Yeah? What's that?" she asked.

"If you're with the one with dashing good looks and a magnetic personality then you have the right guy," I said, breaking into hysterics.

"Well that's a given," she said, leaning over the center console to kiss me on the cheek.

"WOW, I FEEL a little underdressed," Ashlynn said as we walked up the canopied, illuminated sidewalk to Da Vittorio.

"Stop it, you look beautiful as always," I reassured her.

"Welcome to Da Vittorio. May I take your coats?" the host inquired upon our entrance. Handing him our coats, a server guided us to a booth in an intimate corner of the room.

"Have you been here before," he asked.

"No, but I've heard nothing but wonderful things," I said.

"Please take a minute to look over our menu then. We have a varied selection of traditional Italian cuisine as well as many class dishes," he said, placing the menus in front of us. "May I suggest a bottle of house wine for the table?"

"That would be great. Thank you, Andrea," I said, noticing his nametag.

After placing our order, Ashlynn began telling me about her afternoon before asking me again about mine.

"Were you able to reschedule your business trip?"

"Business trip?" I questioned, a bit confused.

"Yeah, the trip you were supposed to take over the weekend. You didn't really tell me much about it. I just assumed it was business-related. Not that you owe me any sort of explanation."

"Oh, yeah, I was supposed to meet with some colleagues at University Hospital in Minneapolis. I haven't decided yet if I'm going to reschedule," I said, providing her with a half-truth.

"I could go along if you want," she blurted out.

"What?"

"Sorry, that was a little presumptuous and rude of me," she apologized.

"No, no, I think that sounds like a great idea. But, could you get away from work?"

"Well, I happen to think my boss might excuse me. But, just so other people wouldn't get the wrong impression and think he was playing favorites, I do have several days of vacation time accrued. I don't remember the last time I took some time off for myself. It would be nice to get away."

"Well OK then. I'll call and schedule the trip tomorrow," I said. "Are you sure though? I might be gone for most of the afternoon. I don't want you to get bored."

"I'll be fine. Didn't you say we'd be in Minneapolis? I'm sure I can take an Uber to the Mall of America. I have a feeling I could easily spend days there."

"OK, it's settled then. I guess we're going to Minneapolis together," I said with a faint smile, uneasy about the awkward situation. Although I looked forward to spending time with Ashlynn alone in a hotel room, I dreaded her learning the real reason behind my trip. Maybe I could keep my secret just a bit longer.

twenty-one

CARSON

*P*ULLING UP TO the hotel, I wished I were more enthusiastic about the getaway with Ashlynn, instead, I dreaded telling her the truth about my business here.

"Oh my gosh, this place is gorgeous! And, I can just walk out of the hotel and into the mall. I think I've died and gone to heaven," Ashlynn said as we checked in with the concierge. I thought I'd surprise her by booking a room at the Marriott hotel, connected to the Mall of America. I knew she was OK with taking an Uber around town, but I didn't feel comfortable with the idea of her being alone in a strange city–call me old-fashioned. "What time is your first appointment? If you have time, we could go check out the mall."

Glancing down at my watch, I knew I only had about thirty minutes to spare before I was scheduled to meet with the director of the long-term care facility. I'd already postponed the meeting once, I didn't want to keep him waiting any longer.

"Sorry, Gorgeous, unfortunately, there's someplace I have to be soon, but I promise I'll be back in time for dinner. Why don't you go check things out? I'll be back in a few hours, and you can tell me all about it," I suggested.

"OK, or I can go with you if you'd like the company?" she asked. "I promise I won't get in your way. You won't even know I'm there."

I still felt horrible for not telling Ashlynn the reason for my visit. I came close to telling her everything on the flight, but then she fell asleep resting against my shoulder and I just couldn't stand the thought of ruining everything that we'd finally built.

"It's OK, you'd probably just be bored anyway. Go enjoy yourself," I said. "Shop till you drop!"

"Ha! Unfortunately, I think my bank account would drop before I would," she laughed.

"Well, then take my AMEX," I said, handing her my card.

"I can't accept that, Carson. I was only kidding anyway. I don't really need to buy that much. Besides, I've turned window shopping into an Olympic sport. One thing I'm actually proud to say I learned from my mother."

"Fine, but if you change your mind, I'll leave this on the counter by the minibar."

WALKING INTO THE long-term care facility, I was overcome with emotion that this could finally be happening for Marissa. Because the receptionist told me that the director would be longer than expected, I asked to see the facility's art room since much of her therapy had revolved around her love of painting.

"May I help you, Sir?" an aide inquired as I entered the room. A few patients sat around the room each working a different project—some sculpting while others painted.

"I hope I'm not disturbing anyone. I just have a friend who was recently accepted as a patient here and I'm just giving myself the ten-cent tour," I explained. "She really enjoys art. I think she'll just love this room with all its vibrant colors," I added, noticing the bright sunlight streaming into the room from the full-length windows.

"No, you're fine," she assured me. "Make yourself at home. As you can see, we don't teach a specific class. We let the patients choose their project."

Perspiration dripped down my forehead as I waited for Marissa to arrive at the gallery. She didn't realize it, but I'd paid for a private viewing of the collection before the show officially opened to the public. She'd been talking about this show for weeks, and I knew this would be the perfect opportunity to finally ask her to be my wife.

I'd been planning this night for several weeks, and finally, it was here. I wanted everything to be perfect—just like her—a night we'd remember on our golden wedding anniversary. We'd talked about marriage while I was in med school, but we agreed then that it'd be better to wait for both of us to graduate and settle into our careers before worrying about the stress of a wedding. I hadn't told her yet about the fellowship I'd been offered, but I hoped she'd be just as excited to move to Texas as I was.

"What are you doing here all alone?" Marissa asked, meeting me in the lobby.

"I paid to rent the gallery for the evening. The staff has already left. It's just us," I explained.

"You did all of this for me?" she gushed. "I can't believe I get to view the artwork before anyone else."

"Enjoy it. You're more than deserve it, Marissa. I'd do it over and over again if it meant I could see that smile on your beautiful face. You light up the room, you know?" I said, embracing her for a gentle kiss. "I have champagne chilling, would you like some?"

"I think that sounds perfect," she said.

After sharing a champagne toast, we walked around the gallery enjoying the various pieces on display. She explained the meaning of each one, smiling vibrantly as she did so. "You can take one of the pieces home," I said.

"Carson, you know I can't afford any of these," she said, shrugging. "It'd be nice if I could though. They're all so beautiful. Maybe someday."

"Marissa, it's my gift to you. I was waiting until the right time to tell you, but I was offered a fellowship in Dallas, and I want you to go with me."

"What?" she asked, unsure of what I was asking.

"Say you'll go with me. I love you, Marissa. Will you be my wife?"

"Oh my god, yes," she squealed, leaping into my arms.

The painting she chose that night still hangs on my office wall—a gentle reminder of how cruel life can be.

AFTER SPENDING THE afternoon touring the long-term care facility and meeting with the team of doctors, including physical and behavioral therapists, and nurses who would be working with Marissa, I was exhausted. Knowing I'd promised to take Ashlynn out for dinner, I hoped she'd be OK with ordering room service and spending the rest of the evening in bed.

Walking into the hotel suite, I was surprised to see Ashlynn already sprawled out across the king-sized bed. She stirred as I crawled into bed next to her. Then she rolled over to face me.

"You really did shop till you dropped, huh?" I laughed, wrapping her tightly in my arms. "I didn't expect to find you here sleeping."

"Yeah, I don't know what's wrong with me," she answered, sleepily. "I didn't even make it to many stores. I'm just exhausted. I hope I'm not coming down with something."

"I'm pretty tired myself. What do you say we just order some room service and stay in tonight?" I suggested.

"That sounds perfect, actually. I bet there are some killer desserts on the menu," she moaned.

"You know, you might feel better if you ate something less sugary," I teased, handing her the menu.

After glancing at it, we ordered a hummus and pita plate, two grilled salmon entrees with roasted fingerling potatoes, and a piece of chocolate fudge cake. For the next hour, we channel surfed as we devoured our meal, propped up on pillows in the luxurious bed.

"I could get used to this," I said before licking a piece of chocolate icing from Ashlynn's lips.

"Mmmm, me too," she moaned.

"I can't believe we just ate all that food though. We aren't going to be able to leave this hotel room all weekend because I'll be in this bed recovering from a food coma. In fact, I think I might just be pregnant with a food baby," she laughed, rubbing her belly.

Just the thought of Ashlynn being pregnant ignited something in me that I'd never felt before. When I'd proposed to Marissa, we were both so young with new, promising careers on the horizon. It's something we wanted, but several years in the future. Now well into my thirties, being a father wasn't something that I'd often thought about. I'd always been Sam's cool uncle, and I was proud to play that role. But now that I'd met Ashlynn, she made the once impossible suddenly seem possible.

"Have you ever thought about having children," I asked, resting my head on her chest.

"No, not really," she sighed heavily. "I suppose I did when I was much younger, but Kyle took away all those dreams."

"He was a sick bastard. It infuriates me that he took so much from you," I said with disgust.

"I'm OK, I've lived with the harsh reality for years. It's just a relief to finally have someone I can confide in."

"You can talk to me about anything," I said, planting another lingering kiss on her lips.

"Thank you, you don't know how much that means to me. I'm there for you too, if you need me?" she questioned. As much as I believed the truth in her words, this time it was me who was holding back.

"Yes, I know," I replied, kissing her along her collarbone.

"As much as I love where this is going, I'd really like to take a shower before bed. Care to join me," she asked, salaciously.

"I have an even better idea. Why don't we take that hot tub for a spin?" I suggested, pointing to the corner of the room.

"I like the way you think."

Turning on the water, I placed my hand under the faucet until it reached just the right temperature. "Ready to hop in with me?" I invited Ashlynn as she sat on the edge of the bed.

"Sure, I just want to freshen up really quick," she said, walking into the bathroom.

Disrobing, I slid into the tub, sinking into the warm water. Resting my head along the edge, I enjoyed the pressure of the jets massaging my back.

"Now don't go falling asleep on me," Ashlynn said as she reentered the room.

Raising my head, she took my breath away in a white, sheer robe which showed off a black lace bra and matching panties.

"Are you trying to kill me coming out here in that sexy number?" I asked. "I nearly drowned."

"You like?" she asked in a sultry tone as she began to slowly loosen the robe.

"Very much, but I'd like it even more if you were naked and riding my cock in this tub," I moaned.

"That can be arranged," she agreed as she unhooked her bra,

her ample chest springing free. Stepping free of her panties, she twirled around, doing her best striptease, showing off her curves before joining me in the tub.

Grabbing her by the waist, I eased her down to my lap where my throbbing cock bobbed between her breasts.

"Carson, I need you," she begged as I positioned her ass against one of the pulsating jets.

"Soon, Gorgeous," I said, kissing her on the forehead before reaching over the edge of the tub to grab a condom from my pants pocket.

"It's fine. I'm on the pill and I haven't been with anyone since I was last tested. Please, trust me?" she asked, sincerely.

"I trust you completely," I said, not wanting her to ever doubt me. "Are you sure this is what you want?"

"Carson, please. I need to feel you. All of you," she begged, the warm water splashing around us.

At her request, I gently guided my cock into her pussy, reveling in the feeling of her walls tightly hugging my thickness. Filling her completely, she rocked back and forth as I pumped my cock back and forth, my balls smacking her ass with each powerful thrust.

Keeping up a vigorous pace for several minutes, I could tell by her breathing that she was getting close to climaxing. Placing my right hand between us, I circled her clit with my thumb just as her pussy began spasming around me.

"Carson, harder. Please," she begged. "I need to come. Please let me come."

"You know you're hot as fuck when you beg," I growled, pumping into her with maximum force. As I came unhinged inside her, she moaned my name before collapsing into my chest.

"That was perfect," she said, her chestnut locks floating freely in the water.

"It was pretty damn hot," I agreed. "But I think we should go warm up under the covers now."

Without giving it a second thought, Ashlynn hopped from the tub dripping wet. "I'll race you," she squealed as droplets of water fell from her perfectly sculpted booty.

"That's not fair!" I yelled. "Your wet, naked body is too much of a distraction."

twenty-two

CARSON

$\mathcal{A}$FTER SPENDING THE entire morning meeting with the medical director of the hospital where I'd be working, I didn't have much time to spare before I had to arrive back to the hotel in time for us to leave for the airport. Knowing my window of opportunity was running out before I had to tell Ashlynn the truth, I made the decision to take her to meet Marissa once we arrived home.

"There's something I need to tell you," I said, shortly before the plane was to land in Detroit.

"I know. I overheard your phone call before we left. I wasn't trying to eavesdrop, but I came back from the pool just as you were accepting the position," Ashlynn confessed.

"You know about the job?" I asked, surprised she waited until now to say anything.

"I'm sorry, I should've told you why I was going to Minneapolis in the first place, but I wasn't sure before we left if I was going to accept the position."

"It's fine. You don't owe me an explanation, Carson," she said, sadness filling her voice. "We haven't been together long. I can't expect you to stay here because of me."

"But what if I wanted to stay right here because of you?"

"I don't understand. I thought you already made the decision to accept the new position?"

"You obviously didn't hear everything then. I told the hospital administrator that I still needed a few days to decide. I wanted to talk to you about it first."

"Well I think you should take it," she said.

"You do?" I questioned, somewhat perplexed.

"Yeah, like I said, we haven't been together for long. You can't put your life and your career on hold just for me." Truthfully, the position wasn't even a step up from my current gig at St. Therese. I'd only be accepting the transfer for one reason and it wasn't to gain another rung on the career ladder.

"It wouldn't be the first time I've put both those things on hold for a woman," I admitted.

"Carson, you aren't making any sense," she said, shaking her head in confusion.

"Before I take you home, there's someplace I need to take you," I said as we began getting off the plane at the airport.

"Sure, I guess," she reluctantly agreed.

Pulling up to the extended-care facility, I turned to face Ashlynn, her eyes revealing uncertainty.

"What are we doing here?" she asked as I parked the SUV.

"I have a friend who's a patient here and I'd like for you to meet her," I explained.

Walking into the facility, I held Ashlynn's hand, hoping she wouldn't leave me after I exposed the truth.

"Carson, it's good to see you. We haven't seen you around

here in a while," Marissa's nurse, Alex, greeted us as we walked through the door.

"Hey Alex! It's good to see you too. I took a new position a few months back, and things have just been really busy for me ever since. Has there been any change in her condition?" I asked, as I always did upon my arrival.

"No, unfortunately, no changes since your last visit. Her primary-care physician has spoken to the neurologist and they've agreed to apply for a new trial study, but the hospital board won't select participants for several more weeks."

"Who's your friend?" Alex inquired upon noticing Ashlynn standing beside me.

"Oh, Alex this is Ashlynn Sommers–my girlfriend," I said, hoping she wouldn't expose too much information to Ashlynn quite yet.

"Oh, I see. It's nice to meet you, Ashlynn," she responded. "Well, you know your way to Marissa's room. If you need anything else, let one of us know."

Making our way down the hallway, Ashlynn stopped me just before we made the turn into Marissa's room.

"Who's Marissa, Carson?" she asked, her eyes pleading for answers. "I have a feeling you're holding something back. She's much more than a friend to you, isn't she?"

"She was my fiancée," I finally had to admit. "She was in the same accident that killed my mother. I actually lost two people who I loved that day."

Ashlynn didn't speak another word before she stepped into Marissa's room. The expression on her face was a mixture of shock and sadness. Marissa was sitting up in a chair, playing with the stuffed bear I'd bought her several years ago. Hearing our footsteps, she turned and looked up at us as we entered the room.

"Carson!" she smiled with glee and waved excitedly when

she saw me. Watching Ashlynn, my heart broke even more as I watched her wipe a single tear from her cheek.

"Hey Marissa! How's my girl doing?" I asked, giving her a peck on the cheek.

"Good! I painted you a picture today," she said, pointing toward a stack of finger paintings.

"Those are all for me?" I asked.

"Yep! I made one each day," she said excitedly.

"I'm sorry I haven't been around to visit a lot lately. I got a new job and I have a new friend who I'd actually like for you to meet," I said, motioning for Ashlynn to come closer.

"Marissa this is Ashlynn. She's a very special lady," I said with a smile.

"Hi Ashley! That's a very pretty name," she said.

"No, no, Marissa. It's . . ."

"It's fine, Carson," Ashlynn interrupted. "It's a pleasure to meet you, Marissa. Your paintings are very beautiful. Do you like art," she asked.

"Yeah," she muttered, nodding her head.

"You should have seen her art before," I mentioned quietly, remembering the time before the accident. "She was working toward her Master of Fine Arts at the time of the accident. Her watercolor paintings were exquisite. She had dreams of opening her own gallery one day."

"I think I need to go get some fresh air," Ashlynn said. "You stay in here with Marissa."

"Ash, I think we should probably go outside and talk."

"Whatever you think is best," she agreed.

"Marissa, we'll be right back, OK," I said, giving her another quick peck on the top of her head.

"OK, see you soon," she said, waving as we exited the room.

After leaving Marissa's room, Ashlynn and I walked in silence outside to the facility's courtyard. For a mid-November afternoon, the weather was quite pleasant. With the sun shining, temperatures were mild for that time of year in Michigan. Some might've even said it was a perfect Indian summer day. Taking a seat on the bench, I was surprised that it felt warm to the touch. "Will you be OK out here?" I asked her, as we took a seat.

"Yes, I'm fine," she said, wrapping her scarf tighter around her neck. "What happened, Carson?" she added, getting right to the point.

"Mom was taking her to pick up her wedding dress since her car was in the shop for maintenance. Coming home from the bridal shop, Mom's car slid off an embankment and hit a tree. Crash-scene investigators found deer tracks in the mud, so they could only conclude that my mom probably swerved to avoid hitting it, and that's when she lost control. She died before paramedics arrived at the scene, but Marissa thankfully survived. She's a stubborn girl, always has been."

"Wow, that's terrible," Ashlynn said, taking my hand in hers. Knowing she was beside me gave me the strength to continue.

"We were supposed to get married a week after the accident, but she was still in a coma. Once she came out of it, I wanted to marry her right there in the hospital room, but her parents thought we should wait until she could go home. But that was over ten years ago, and she hasn't been able to go home—she probably never will.

"I promised her on the day that should've been our wedding day that once she was well enough, I'd give her the big, fancy wedding that she'd always dreamed of."

"Will she ever fully recover?" Ashlynn asked, her voice barely above a whisper.

"Hard to say. The human body is such a mystery—you know that as well as anyone. She's been through several clinical trials over the last ten years, but nothing has seemed to help much. Dealing with a traumatic brain injury is a beast on its own. Her cognitive abilities are those of a preschooler."

"So, she's the reason you're still single then? Not your job like you've been telling me all along?" Ashlynn asked, a hint of disappointment in her tone.

"Yes and no," I admitted, knowing she deserved a better explanation. "For many years, yes, I didn't date because of Marissa. I became her primary caregiver because her parents didn't have the means to cover her medical expenses as easily as I could. They didn't turn down my offer because I felt as though they held me partially responsible. I buried myself in my work, and I was content with my decisions. I'm sorry I didn't tell you the whole truth. You deserved the truth from me, especially since I asked for so much of it from you."

"It's OK, I get it. I definitely didn't make it easy for you to open up to me when I kept my own secrets hidden for so long," she said comfortingly. "And, you can't really believe that the accident is in any way your fault," she added, shaking her head.

As much as I realized she was right, part of me would always blame myself for the accident. Had I not been so focused on that fellowship, I would've taken the time out of my schedule to drive her to the bridal shop myself. My mother would still be alive, and I'd be a married man with children of my own.

"She wouldn't have been rushing about to get her wedding dress that day if it weren't for me. I'd just completed my residency and was offered a fellowship opportunity in Dallas that I couldn't pass up. Marissa agreed to move up the wedding, so she could go with me. She asked me to take her that day instead of Mom, but I was too busy finalizing our plans for the move."

"I'm so sorry you've had to deal with all of this for so long," Ashlynn said. "You know it's not your fault, right?"

"Yes, I know, but it doesn't hurt any less," I confessed. "The kicker in the whole, fucked-up situation was that the wedding dress went perfectly unscathed in the backseat of the car. Not even one fucking sequin was out of place."

"So, you're unsure about taking the job in Minneapolis because of Marissa then?" she asked, still unclear about our future together. Taking a deep breath, I braced myself for Ashlynn's possible reaction.

"No, I would accept the job because of Marissa. If I rejected the offer it would be because of you."

"What? I don't understand."

"I've been trying to get Marissa into a state-of-the-art facility that specializes in traumatic brain injuries ever since the accident occurred. There are only three in the country and five in the entire world that fit the exact type of care that we've been seeking all these years. There's a facility in Minneapolis that finally approved of admitting her as a patient. It just so happens that the hospital affiliated with the facility has an opening in its psychiatric department. I would move there to oversee her care."

"And, what would I have to do with you staying?" she asked with hope-filled eyes.

"I care about you so much, Ashlynn," I said. "I never thought I wanted to find someone other than Marissa, but that all changed the day I met you. I knew from the moment I first laid my eyes on you that you were someone special. All along, I thought I was the one saving you from your demons when you were actually the one saving me from mine.

"I've wanted this for Marissa for so long, but now that it's here, I'm not sure I can go. I just don't think I can leave you behind. I know that sounds incredibly selfish of me."

"Do you still love her, Carson?" Ashlynn questioned, her lip beginning to quiver like it does when she's about to cry.

"I think a part of me will always love her," I admitted, hoping Ashlynn wasn't hurt by my truth.

"Then you need to go," she said, squeezing my hand. "As much as I don't want to lose you, I don't want to be the reason you stay here either."

This didn't seem like the appropriate time or place to tell her, but there was something else she needed to hear. "I wasn't quite done yet, Ash. A part of me might always love Marissa, but I'm in love with you. I love you, Ashlynn Sommers."

"What?" she stammered.

"I love you," I whispered, realizing she hadn't repeated the words.

"I care about you so much, Carson, but I still think you need to go," she whispered. "I don't want to become a regret someday. Please accept the position–for me–and for Marissa."

"Will you come with me?" I asked, praying she would accept my offer.

"You know I can't do that. I have a job here. Family here. My entire life is in Michigan. Besides, I'm not sure Bradley Cooper could function for five minutes without me," she laughed, wiping the fresh tears from her eyes.

Dropping my head to my knees, I wasn't sure how to react to her selflessness. All this time, I was worried about her running when I told her my secrets, but instead, she'd been so incredibly brave and understanding. I knew I definitely loved this woman, but I knew telling her the words would've only crushed her.

"You know, you're a pretty remarkable woman, Ashlynn Sommers," I said, pulling her into my chest.

"You're pretty great yourself, Carson Foster," she said, snuggling into the crook of my arm. "It's going to be so hard to say goodbye. When do you have to leave?"

"The job starts the first week in December. I need to schedule

Marissa's transport for the day after Thanksgiving. I'd like to see that she gets settled into her new home before I have to worry about the new position."

"So, that's just four days from now," she said, counting with her fingers.

"Yeah, that seems about right," I said, exhaling sharply. Why, if this was the right thing to do, did it hurt so fucking bad?

"Well, we'll still be able to spend Thanksgiving together. And, if it's all right with you, maybe I can fly out for Christmas and New Year's? My mother may disown me for not spending the holidays with her and Daddy, but eventually she'll get over it," she mused.

"I think that sounds absolutely wonderful. I want nothing more than for this to work between us, Ashlynn. I know long-distance relationships can be hard, but I want to try."

"Me too," she said, placing a soft kiss on my cheek. "Now, as much as I wish we could sit out here forever, I think my toes are starting to freeze," she teased.

twenty-three

ASHLYNN

*I*T WAS HOURS before sunrise, and here I was wide awake with my arms stuffed elbows deep inside Mr. Tom Turkey.

"Whose idea was it again to host Thanksgiving dinner this year?" I asked Carson as he poured himself a fifth cup of coffee.

"Yours? Maybe mine? Hell, I don't know. We're both fucking idiots," he groaned, stumbling his way to the kitchen table.

"You do realize you're leaving tomorrow, and we could've just spent the whole day alone in bed eating junk food, watching movies, and having sex and no one would've bothered us at all, right?" I asked, wishing we'd taken that route instead of the one that involved inviting a dozen of our closest family and friends to my home for Thanksgiving and for Carson's going-away party.

"Oh god, when you put it that way, we just sound like even bigger idiots," he laughed. "I know, let's just call them all right now and cancel. Then we can spend the entire day in bed snogging."

"Snogging?" I chuckled. "I thought you were moving to Minnesota, not England?"

"You know you find my British accent sexy," he joked, snuggling into the crook of my neck.

"You really need to get some sleep. You're acting all sorts of crazy right now."

"I think you're probably right. I don't think I've gotten more than two hours sleep over the last week." We'd spent the last few days packing up Carson's apartment, so everything would be ready when the movers were scheduled to arrive bright and early in the morning.

"Go back to sleep. I have everything handled out here. Brad should be here soon anyway. He said he doesn't trust me to cook a proper Thanksgiving meal for everyone."

"OK, if you insist," he agreed. "But, just remember, there's still time to call this whole thing off, should you change your mind and want to join me in bed."

"YOU SURE YOU didn't accidentally poison any of the food?" Brad asked, sliding the Jell-O mold he'd made into the fridge.

"No, just the ToFurkey I made especially for you," I quipped, rolling my eyes at Brad.

"Aww, you actually made it? You really do love me," he gushed.

"Mmmm, I'd call it more of a moment of weakness."

"So, Carson really is leaving tomorrow, huh?" he questioned.

"Yeah, I'm trying not to think about it. It just hurts too damn much. I finally let someone into my life and now he's leaving," I sighed.

"Ask him not to leave?" Brad suggested.

"No, I can't do that. This is the right thing for him and Marissa. She needs him more than I do," I said, not really believing my words.

"Do you really think you can handle a long-distance relationship?" Brad asked.

"I don't know. I told him I'd at least try. I honestly don't see how it can work though if neither one of us plans on leaving though," I said, shrugging. "I just don't know what to do because I really am falling for him, Brad."

"Ashlynn Renee Sommers, do you love him?"

"Yes," I sighed. "I'm definitely falling in love with him."

"No matter what happens, I'm proud of you," he said, hugging me tightly. "This is such a selfless thing for you to do. My Ashlynn has flown the nest."

"You're such a turd. I was actually being serious and opening up to you!" I sassed, throwing a dish towel at his face. "Just for that, you get to help me with the giblets."

"Eww, I can't believe you even kept those slimy things," he said, scrunching his nose in disgust.

PULLING THE TURKEY out of the oven, the doorbell rang alerting me that the first of our guests had arrived. "I'll get it," I heard Carson yell from the living room where he and Brad had been watching football.

"Hi Honey," Mom said, waltzing into the kitchen carrying a boatload of extra food.

"Hi Mom," I said, taking the dishes from her hands as she pecked me on the cheek.

"That new boyfriend of yours sure is a good-looking fella," Mom whispered into my ear. "And, a doctor. Don't do anything to scare this one away."

"Thanks, Mom. I'll try not to, but like I told you on the phone, he accepted a position in Minneapolis and is leaving tomorrow."

"And, why aren't you going with him?" she asked, nosily.

"Please don't nag me today, Mom," I pleaded. "I just want this to be the perfect Thanksgiving. I know that's probably asking a lot, but please try–for me."

"Sure, Dear, I'll try. Now, I sure hope you have a lot more guests coming because we have enough food here to feed an entire army."

"Just Carson's brother and nephew. Why did you bring so much extra food anyway?"

"Because Bradley called me yesterday and said I might want to bring back up," she giggled.

"Bradley Cooper! Get in here, right now!" I demanded, yelling into the living room.

"Coming," he shouted. "Thank god you called me in here, lord knows I was only watching football to catch the halftime show."

"Why did you tell my mom to bring extra food? I told you I had it covered," I snapped.

"Sorry, I was just covering the bases," he said with a shrug.

"Hey! Look who finally showed up?" Carson said as Camden and Sam walked into the room behind him.

"Hey guys! Guess what, thanks to Brad and my mother we're going to start a new Thanksgiving tradition! Since we have more food here than we know what to do with, I was thinking we could all go to the soup kitchen before we come back here and have dinner," I suggested.

"I think that sounds like the perfect holiday tradition, Gorgeous. Almost as good as the Christmas tradition we've already started this year," he flirted, placing a kiss to the tip of my nose.

Returning from a day at the soup kitchen, we came home to eat our very own Thanksgiving meal. I even managed to cook the entire meal without burning an entire thing. Even Brad complimented me on my cooking. It was the perfect holiday except for the fact that Carson would be gone in less than twenty-four hours.

ONE WEEK HAD passed since Carson moved to Minneapolis. He'd gotten Marissa settled into the new facility and she seemed to be thriving in the new environment–especially with the expanded art therapy treatment. I missed him like crazy, but he'd called me nearly every night which had helped to somewhat ease the pain. Thinking that I hadn't heard from him yet today, I pulled out my phone to send him a quick message.

ASHLYNN: *Hey, I miss you. I thought I would've heard from you by now.*

CARSON: *Hey, Gorgeous, I was just thinking about you. I hate to do this, but I don't think I'll be able to talk tonight. It's been a crazy day and I still have a few hours left here at the hospital. Call you tomorrow?*

ASHLYNN: *Yeah, sure. I understand. I wanted to talk to you about Christmas though. Do you have any vacation days? I just didn't know how long I should stay.*

CARSON: *I don't think I'm going to have much time, but we can talk about it tomorrow. I love you.*

ASHLYNN: *OK. I love you too.*

Tossing my phone back in my purse, I was slightly disappointed by our exchange. It was the first time since Carson left that I felt like he hadn't made time for me. Before I had a chance to feel too sorry for myself there was a light knock on my office door.

"Come in," I yelled, assuming it was Brad.

"Hey, I brought you a surprise, but you need to close your eyes," Brad said, stepping into my office.

"OK," I said, skeptically. Hearing the shuffling of feet, it took all my willpower not to open my eyes. "Can I open them yet?" I pleaded.

"Just a few more seconds," he said.

"OK, you can open them now," a familiar voice said.

"Carson?" I asked. "Is that really you?"

"It's me, Gorgeous. Open your eyes and see for yourself."

Opening my eyes, I was shocked to see Carson kneeling in front of my chair holding open a ring box. Inside the box was the most exquisite, solitaire diamond.

"What's that?" I gasped.

"It's an engagement ring, Ash. I want nothing more than for you to be my wife. Ashlynn Renee Sommers, will you marry me?

"Eeeeep! Say yes," I heard Brad squeal from out in the hallway.

"I don't understand, I thought you were in Minneapolis. Why are you back here?"

"After just the first day, I knew I couldn't be away from you. I made sure Marissa settled into the new facility, and I came home. I can visit her every few months. She'll be fine there without me."

"What about your job?"

"I called Joleen, and she doesn't plan on coming back to St. Therese. The position was mine if I wanted it. I came in earlier today to sign the contract."

"So, you're back? For good?"

"Yes, now say 'yes' already!"

"YES!" I shrieked, leaping into his arms as he smothered me with kisses.

ASHLYNN
Five Years Later . . .

"**I** CAN'T BELIEVE you talked me into getting the biggest Christmas tree on the lot," Carson grumbled, opening the door of the minivan. "I'm going to have to call Cam to help me get the damn thing up. I'm getting too old for this, Ash."

"You're the one who wanted the tradition of a real Christmas tree. And, you know the kids are going to pick the biggest one! After all, we have the largest selection on the first of November!" I reminded him, pulling Savannah's car seat from the back. "It's not my fault if the kids expect it now."

"They're too little to know any better. I doubt either of them would even realize it next year. You always talk about wanting one of those pink metallic trees. We can start a new tradition. I'm sure Savannah would just love that when she gets older."

"I know, Daddy," Gabe said, pulling on Carson's leg. "Can we go see Santa now?"

"Not yet, Buddy," he said, patting him on the top of the head. "Breakfast with Santa isn't until morning."

"Pancakes for breakfast, Daddy?" Gabe asked.

"I'm sure there will be pancakes, Bud," he answered, patiently. Carson was such a good father. He was just as understanding and caring with our children as he'd been with me all those years ago.

"With chocolate chips, Daddy?" I couldn't help but laugh at my son's question.

"Ashlynn! What are you teaching our children?" Carson yelled.

"Breakfast for dessert, Baby. I can't be blamed for teaching our children logic," I laughed, pecking him on the lips.

CARSON

"DID CAMDEN AND Sam leave?" Ashlynn asked as I walked back into the living room. "I was just about to boil a pot of hot chocolate."

"Yeah, Sam has hockey practice early in the morning."

"Oh, OK, that's too bad. The kids would've loved it if they could've stayed."

"Cam promised they'd all come back before Christmas," I told her.

"Mommy, can we open our presents now?" Gabe asked from beside the tree. After Cam helped me get it up and into its tree stand, Ashlynn and Gabe started hanging the ornaments as Savannah napped in her pack 'n play.

"Not all of them, Baby," she said, shaking her head. "That one is for Daddy anyway. Can you give the present to Daddy?"

"Here, Daddy," Gabe said as I took the wrapped package out of his chubby, little hands.

"Open it," she said slyly as if she'd been keeping a secret.

Ripping open the box, I pulled out our family's annual Christmas ornament. The same ornament I'd promised Ashlynn the first year we'd met.

Looking at the glass bulb, upon first glance, I noticed a family of snowmen with each of our names written under each snow person and kitties: Daddy, Mommy, Gabe, Savannah, Steve Urkel, and Fresh Prince. What I failed to notice the first time was the word "baby" written in the belly of the mommy snowman.

"Wait. Are you pregnant?" I asked in shock. After we had Savannah, we decided we were happy with two children. A healthy baby boy and girl–what more could we possibly ask for?

"I am," she said, a smile forming on her lips.

"Are you sure?"

"Yes, I took a test last week. I went to the doctor today to confirm it. I'm due in early June," she said, excitedly.

"This is the perfect gift," I exclaimed. "I love it and you."

"I love you too."

"Now, let's put the kids to bed so we can take care of the third part of our yearly Christmas tradition. I plan on making love to my pregnant wife under that tree all night long," I whispered into her ear, placing a chaste kiss on her forehead.

acknowledgments

FIRST AND FOREMOST, I want to thank my readers—you amaze me every single day. Without you, I wouldn't have continued on this writing journey. Your daily messages over the last four years have been the highlight of many of my days. The friendships I have made with many of you, I know will last a lifetime. For that, I'm truly grateful. I've said it before and I'll say it again, there are so many wonderful books to choose from and I'm truly honored that you took the time to read mine. Thank you for the bottom of my heart!

To my beta readers: Johnaka McCosker and Tammi Hart— thank you for helping me dig deeper and making Take Me There a much more polished story. You answered my unending questions and, in the process, have become some of my dearest friends. Thank you and I love you all more than you will ever know!

To Johnaka McCosker: Thank you for giving this PA thing a whirl with me and for keeping me on my toes–or trying to at least–on a daily basis. My days would be incomplete without our daily chats and gif messages.

To Christina Rhoads: Thank you for just being you. Thank you for giving me a hard time at every opportunity for not writing this book faster. I may have pretended to hate it, but deep down it gave me the motivation to continue. Thank you for loving my stories and my characters more than I think I even do at times–more like all the time. I could go on and on, but just know you are a truly special person and deserve the very best out of life–don't ever think otherwise . . . EVER! I love you!

Christina Gipson: Thank you for being the morning person to my night owl. I love our crazy adventures, and I can't wait to see what the next one brings. #NoBitch

Margaret, Missy, Lisa, Christine, Stacy, Kristy, Norma, Norma, Kim, Christina, and Christina: thank you for your support and encouragement while we were in Chicago. Spending the weekend with you all gave me the encouragement I needed to keep writing this book. Thank you to all of you for giving me the swift kick I needed to get my booty in gear!

To Kylie and staff at Give Me Books—thank you for helping me with the behind-the-scenes work with my release blitz. You have no idea how much your support means to me.

To all of the amazing ladies who worked to beautify Take Me There: my fabulous cover designer, Michele Catalano, for taking my visions and turning them into realities; Jean Woodfin of JW Photography and Covers for the beautiful cover photo—you truly are such a talent and an absolute pleasure to work with. I knew when I saw this photo that these two were my vision of Carson and Ashlynn. I look forward to working with you on future projects; and Christine Borgford of Type A Formatting for the stunning inside formatting—thank you for always helping me in any way that you possibly can! You've been with me since the very beginning and I can't imagine this journey without you in it.

To some of the most incredible indie authors I've met during this journey–In an attempt to not miss anyone, I'll simply say you know who you are! Thank you for your stories, advice, and friendship. There aren't enough words to express my appreciation. Love you all!

To the bloggers who have shared in the cover reveal, reviewed and promoted Take Me There—none of this would be possible without your constant hard work and dedication. Your support humbles me on a daily basis—thank you!

To, my husband, Brian: Thank you for your "support" during my writing journey. For listening to me whine, putting up with the sink full of dishes (and even doing them a time or two), and the piles of unfolded laundry while I'm on deadline–and all the other times. I love you!

To my dad: Thank you and your librarian ways for showing me at a young age that books could be pretty cool. And, thank you for reading my words! You've always supported my ideas, some crazier than others, and I'll be forever grateful. I love you!

Please feel free to join my Facebook group, M.C. Decker's Books, to talk about Unforeseen as well as other books by M.C. Decker. www.facebook.com/groups/MCDeckersBooks

about the author

M.C. DECKER IS the Top 100 Bestselling author who loves to write stories of true love and second chances. She lives in a suburb of Flint, Michigan with her husband, Brian, and spoiled-rotten Siamese cat, Simon. For the last decade, she has worked as a journalist for several community newspapers in Michigan. She enjoys all things '80s and '90s pop culture: movies, boy bands, music and especially the color, hot pink. She also strictly lives by the motto, "Life is better in flip flops," and is a diehard Detroit Tigers fan.

also by
M.C. DECKER

UNSPOKEN SERIES
Unwritten
Unscripted
The Unwritten Duet Box Set
Unwrapped (holiday novella)
Unforeseen

STANDALONES
Love Entwined
Forever Entwined (A Love Entwined novella)